CLAIMED

ICE WORLD WARRIORS : BOOK 1

JESSICA GRAYSON

ARIA WINTER

Purple Fall
Publishing

Published in the United States by Purple Fall Publishing. Purple Fall Publishing and the Purple Fall Publishing Logos are trademarks and/or registered trademarks of Purple Fall Publishing LLC.

ISBN 978-164-253-1787 ebook

978-164-253-0124 paperback

Cover Design by Maria Spada

PRINTED IN THE UNITED STATES OF AMERICA

Dedication

DEDICATION

To my husband: You are not just my husband, you are my best friend and my rock. Thank you for all your love and support. I love you more than words can ever say.

-Jessica Grayson

CHAPTER 1

LARA

A low, hissing noise startles me awake. My eyes snap open and my pulse pounds in my ears as blinding, bright light floods my vision. I squeeze them shut against the assault and carefully squint, trying to take in my surroundings.

Where am I?

The last thing I remember is going to sleep in one of the stasis pods on the way back to Terra from Mars. I've made the round trip before to the red planet, but I've never woken up like this. Usually, it's a gentle and gradual awakening, accompanied by some Beethoven, or something equally soothing, to allow us to transition easier from deep sleep to complete wakefulness.

A loud hiss in my left ear draws my attention. Something cold and wet slicks up my neck, and I jerk my head to the side.

My eyes widen, and I'm paralyzed with fear as two enormous black orbs with red, vertically slit pupils study me intently.

With a hooded face, like a cobra, it's covered in shiny, crimson, interlocking scales. The creature's lips pull back in a snarl, baring two long fangs as a red, forked tongue retracts into its mouth.

The creature boasts two arms, two legs, and a long, tapered tail. Thick layers of muscle line its sinuous form.

Ice cold fear floods my veins when I notice the large bulge beneath his pants, between his legs. He leans in, studying me intently with a look akin to lust.

I try to jerk away, but my limbs won't respond. I glance down at my form. I'm in a paper-thin gown, that only goes to mid-thigh, and suspended in some kind of force field.

The alien extends his black claws and rips a line down the fabric, tearing it off me. Cold air prickles my skin, and I shiver as overwhelming fear takes hold.

I scan the room for anyone else, wondering where the rest of my crew is, but I don't see them. Shiny, metal panels line the floors, walls, and ceiling. I stare in horror at my reflection. My long, brown hair is disheveled and loose from my braid. My gray-blue eyes are wide with fear, my entire body trembling as the alien begins to circle me.

"Who are you? What do you want?"

He bares his fangs and responds with several elongated hissing sounds.

A door on the opposite wall slides open, and another snake alien enters, looking to the first one. They speak to each other in a language I cannot possibly hope to under-stand. After a moment, they both turn to face me.

The second one picks up a small instrument of some kind and moves in my direction. A tear slips down my cheek as he walks behind me, the press of cold metal coming to rest behind my ear.

A sharp sting pierces my skin. Warmth blooms out from the site, building into a fire so intense I can barely breathe.

The alien leans in. "Do you understand what I'm saying?"

Blinding pain shoots through my skull. I can hardly think much less form any words.

He grabs my chin in a bruising grip, forcing my gaze to his. "Can you understand me?" he grinds out.

"Yes," I somehow manage to whisper as my eyes roll up in the back of my head, and I fall away into a darkened void.

Awareness slowly trickles back into my mind as I open my eyes to near-total darkness. I reach out and my hand hits cold, hard metal grating. Adrenaline rushes through my system as I remember where I am.

Lost. On an alien ship. I'm a prisoner. Or—I survey my form, adjusting to the dim lighting—judging by what I have on and the way I was treated... I'm a slave.

I reach behind my ear, lightly tracing a tiny metal stud protruding from my skin. It must be some sort of translator, since I was able to understand the alien after he gave it to me. The echoes of remembered pain whisper across my flesh, and I wince at the tenderness that still remains.

Turning to the left, I notice another set of bars—a cage. Inside, a woman with long, blonde hair lies completely still on the floor.

"Hello?" I call out.

Slowly, she turns to face me, her eyes going wide as they meet mine. She jerks up. "You're Terran?"

"Yes."

Two sharp, brown eyes behind her draw my attention, and my mouth drifts open when I realize it's a golden retriever. "You have a dog with you?"

As if knowing I'm talking about it, the dog wags its tail excitedly, moving to her side and leaning into her. "Yes," she strokes its fur. "This is Barkli. She was with me when I"—she stops abruptly as if searching for the right words before finally saying—"when we were taken... or abducted. Or... I'm not sure what. I just know we went to sleep on the way back to Terra from Mars and woke up in some sort of alien hell."

I quickly inspect the room around us and clench my jaw. *She's right. This is hell.*

"I'm Lara Martin. What's your name?"

"I'm Amanda Knight."

My jaw drops. "Did you say 'Amanda Knight'?"

Her brow furrows softly. "Yes."

I scan her again from head to toe. "You—you look so young."

"I hope so." She frowns. "I'm only twenty-five."

I shake my head. This cannot be real. This has to be a dream—a nightmare of some sort. I pinch my arm, trying to wake myself up, just to be sure.

No luck.

I move closer, eyeing her intently. "You've been gone for over a decade."

Her mouth drifts open, and she blinks at me in astonishment. "What?"

"Your ship. The *Navis*. It disappeared over a decade ago. You and the rest of your crew. Liana Garza, Jeff—"

"Do you know where they are?"

"No.... I don't even know where *my* crew is."

Absently petting the dog, her head drops toward the floor with a faraway look. "Over a decade," she murmurs in a voice so low I almost miss it. She lifts her eyes to mine. "How is that possible?"

"I-I don't know."

"My parents? My sister? Are they all right?"

I shake my head. "I don't know. The families of the crew gather every year at the launch site on the anniversary of your ship's disappearance, but I don't know anything about them specifically."

"How did you get here?" she asks. "What's the last thing you remember?"

"Going to sleep in the stasis pod on the way back to Terra from Mars."

A tear slips down her cheek. "Just like me."

She stills with the sound of booted steps echoing down the corridor. She pulls herself to the cage bars, forlornly placing her palm against the metal grating.

So glad to have found another Terran, I place my palm to hers as she whispers urgently. "The masters are coming. They think we're V'loryns."

I blink at her. "V'loryns? What are—"

"There isn't time to explain," she says. "Just go along with it. Never let anyone think you are different. As far as they are concerned, you're a V'loryn."

"But... why?"

"V'loryn females are one of the most valuable species on the slave markets. They won't sell them to any but the highest bidder, and they won't allow clients to pay to have sex with you. They're also hesitant to use the shock sticks on us."

Panic tightens my chest. "So we *are* slaves?" I ask, just to be sure. I'd already suspected, but to hear the things she's saying, I pray to God it isn't true.

"Just remember. You're V'loryn. The snake guys are Anguis. The insectoids are Zovians."

I stare at her in disbelief. "Insectoids?"

The doors whoosh open, and two Anguis appear. One of them darts his forked tongue out, scenting the air. He taps some sort of short metal rod on the floor. As it begins a low, buzzing hum, my heart stops at the realization of what it is.

This is the shock stick Amanda warned me about.

"Come along," he hisses as he grabs my arm and jerks me out of the cage.

The floor is cold beneath my feet as Amanda and I are escorted down the hall with Barkli padding along beside her.

My nose wrinkles at the putrid stench wafting through the air.

I glance down at Barkli. She regards the two aliens warily, but because Amanda has tight control of her collar, she doesn't do more than bare her teeth and snarl occasionally.

Walking down the corridor, we pass row upon row of dark cages. Several sets of eyes stare back at us from the darkness. Creatures of all shapes and sizes—aliens, I realize —are all crammed together, unlike the cages Amanda and I just came from. Her words repeat in my mind: *V'loryns are more valuable.*

I guess that explains why they had us in cages a bit larger than these.

I want to ask where we're going, but since Amanda says nothing, I follow her lead. Despite my fear, I force myself to focus, taking note of each turn and door we enter, hoping it will somehow help if we manage to escape later.

We stop in front of an airlock door, and my eyes meet Amanda's. Wherever we are, we're far away from home. The realization hits me with a finality that settles in my chest like a heavy stone. No help is coming. If we're going to escape, we're going to have to save ourselves.

The door opens with a sharp hiss. A noxious scent fills the air, so thick I can taste it on my tongue. I thought the stench was bad on the ship, but this is much worse. I glance down at poor Barkli. Dogs have a much more acute sense of smell than Terrans. I can only imagine how horrible this is for her sensitive nose.

As we walk down the ramp, I scan the dozens of ships docked nearby. All shapes and sizes occupy the hangar, some appearing so rusted and worn down I wonder how they're even space-worthy. But there are many others that appear rather formidable—with sleek designs and weapons' cannons along their hulls.

I dart a glance around the space, hoping to find a window or porthole of some sort to check the stars, searching for anything familiar, but everything is entirely enclosed by metal panels, and I can see nothing of the outside.

An alien lizard-man with dark-green scales runs up to our captors and asks if they'd like to have the ship refueled. His long, tapered tail drags on the floor behind him.

I shudder inwardly when I notice the two rows of sharp fangs lining his mouth as he speaks.

His yellow, vertically slit pupils expand as he looks over Amanda and me. He may not be Terran, but it is easy to read the lust in his glare. He turns his attention back to our 'masters.' "How much for time with the females?"

The one behind me bares his fangs in a sharp hiss. "Since when can a Lacerta afford to buy time with V'loryn slaves?" he sneers. "They already have a buyer waiting for their delivery."

Amanda and I exchange a worried glance, but remain silent. We've already been sold, and we're on our way to be delivered to new masters. Tears sting my eyes and blur my vision, but I blink them back. Crying won't do any good.

I can't afford to break down. I draw in several deep breaths, forcing myself to focus and remembering my training.

I'm a Navigator in the Terran Space Program. We're taught how to handle stress through countless simulations.

After all, no one wants an emergency situation to lead to catastrophic failure because the crew freezes in panic when something unforeseen occurs.

Studying our surroundings, I make a mental note of every detail as we step out of the hangar and onto a promenade.

Rusted and worn metal panels line the floors, walls, and ceiling. Several vendors peddling their wares stand outside their run-down shops, calling out to capture the attention of potential customers.

I note several different aliens. With tails, fangs, feathers, horns, scales and wings, aliens of all shapes, sizes and colors make up the crowd, many of them openly staring at me and Amanda as we pass.

My first inclination is to call out for help, but when I notice another alien, ahead of us, dragging a collared slave behind him, I realize that no one here cares about our plight.

At least... not enough to actually try to do anything about it.

I used to imagine first contact with another species would be this amazing and wonderful thing—to know Terrans weren't alone in the universe. That there were others out there searching for life, just like we were.

But I was wrong. Life out here is not what I pictured. It's dark and cold and vile, a nightmare I never considered when I joined the Terran space program.

How naïve I was to think such darkness wouldn't exist out here in the void?

Bright, flashing signs assault my vision with symbols and strange lettering I can't understand. Apparently, these translators only work for speech not written language. As we pass one establishment, my stomach drops. Even though I can't read the sign above the door, I know exactly what this place is.

It's a pleasure house. My heart hammers in my chest as

our masters lead us inside. Vacantly eying the room, I swallow against the bile rising in the back of my throat. Several thick, plush sofas are spread out throughout the space. Customers and slaves—all of them alien—are practically crammed together in this establishment.

It's easy to tell who the clients are, as they hold tight to the chains of the collared slaves forced to either sit at their sides or on their laps. As our captors lead us past them, I notice several of them stop and stare open-mouthed at Amanda and me.

Several hushed whispers follow us as they guide us through another door and into a hallway.

"V'loryns," I hear someone murmur.

"How did they get them?"

"Risky, but profitable," another voice says. "I'm going to try buying some time with them."

My stomach twists in a violent knot at the last sentence. Peering in the direction of the voice, I notice a lizard man, similar to the one we first saw when we stepped off the ship. He smirks sickeningly, his green, reptilian eyes traveling up and down my form.

I look away in a shudder.

The hallway is poorly lit and lined with several doors. A woman's voice cries out from within one of the rooms, the sound cut off by a bestial roar. A rhythmic thumping begins, followed by pitiful whimpers.

Goosebumps prickle my flesh, the understanding of what those sounds mean filling me with unbridled panic.

Without thinking, I take Amanda's hand and squeeze it tight. She does the same as we're guided farther down the hallway.

When we reach a door at the end, they open it and lead us through, but I don't see anything here. Not even a bed. There is nothing but a floor-to-ceiling, dark curtain along the far wall.

"Take off your clothes."

Paralyzing fear snakes through me.

Oh god, are they going to rape us?

"Take. Off. Your. Clothes," the other Anguis asserts, with a sickening smirk, "or we will remove them for you."

I look to Amanda, and it's easy to see, even as concerned as she is, she's even more worried about Barkli. Despite the fear behind her eyes, she moves calmly to unfasten the clasps of her slave gown. The golden retriever watches her intently; the dog is not easily fooled, but she's trained well enough to understand Amanda doesn't want her to cause trouble.

Amanda removes her clothes and stands calmly before the Anguis as I remove mine. For all that Amanda tries to project a calm outer demeanor, Barkli begins making a low whine in the back of her throat while watching Amanda. Dogs are intelligent, and it's obvious she understands something is wrong.

We each try to cover our breasts and pelvic area with our hands. The masters hiss and jerk our arms away from our bodies. "The buyers must be able to see you," one of them seethes. "Now, hold out your arms."

I lift my trembling arms out to my sides. One of them kicks at my foot, gesturing for me to widen my stance. My heart pounds as he runs a strange wand over my body. My skin heats beneath the bright light it emits, a burning sensation traveling over my flesh like I've scrubbed myself raw.

A pained whimper escapes me, but I bite my lower lip when the Anguis growls low in his throat. "Be quiet while we clean you."

When he's done, not a speck of dirt, grime, or sweat remains on my body. The Anguis push us toward the curtain.

"Stand straight," one of them commands. "Let them look at you."

I want to ask who he's talking about but think better of it when his yellow eyes meet mine, baring his fangs with an angry hiss.

The curtain slides back, and I blink several times against the bright light flooding my vision. I squint against the harsh assault, unable to see anything beyond. Barkli's lips pull back in a feral snarl, a low growl rumbling in her chest. Whatever is beyond the lights, she doesn't like it.

"Barkli," Amanda whispers urgently. "Quiet."

The retriever instantly goes silent.

"You see, potential buyers"—a voice calls out over a speaker—"this V'loryn female comes with a companion animal to guard her so you need not worry about others stealing her away."

'Potential buyers...'

Fear trickles down my spine.

I turn to Amanda. Her eyes are wide, and I'm certain her panicked expression mirrors my own.

A murmur of voices fills the air, some of them accented by elongated hissing sounds similar to the Anguis while others are punctuated by growls and harsh clicks. I wonder how many aliens are out there bidding on us right now.

The curtain slides back into place, and a strong hand grips my shoulder, pulling me back. I spin to find the Anguis. "Come on. We don't have much time. Your new master is waiting."

I turn to Amanda and watch in horror as she and Barkli are being led in the opposite direction. "Wait," I stop, digging my heels into the floor. "Why are you separating us?"

"You've been sold to different buyers," he sneers.

My jaw drops when the other Anguis snaps a collar around Amanda's neck and yanks on the chain. "Let's go!"

"Wait!" I cry out, struggling to free myself from his grasp. Cold metal settles heavily around my neck, followed by the harsh click of my collar being secured. My pulse pounds in my ears as I rush toward her, desperately grabbing her hand, holding tightly to her until she's ripped from me and pulled into the doorway.

A violent jerk on my chain makes me stumble backward and fall to the ground.

Tears flood my vision as I helplessly watch her get taken away. Her eyes meet mine. "Be strong," she whispers before the door slams closed behind her.

"No!" I wail, clawing desperately at my collar. "Let me go!"

Another wrenching tug on the chain pulls me back against the hard wall of his chest. Snarling, he grabs my chin in a bruising grip, baring two long fangs dripping with venom. "Calm, or I will make you calm."

I instantly go still, my heart beating wildly in my chest. His tongue snakes out and licks the side of my face, eyes rolling up in the back of his head, relishing the taste of my skin. His lips pull back in a sinister grin. "Come. Your new master awaits."

He leads me through another door.

A man with pale green skin and white hair walks toward me. With pointed, elvish ears and aristocratic features, he looks just like one of the Elves of ancient Terran lore. He has three slight cranial ridges that start between his brows—one going straight up to his hairline, the other two spreading out like a V to his temples.

His glowing green eyes study me with an ice-cold gaze. "What are you?" His deep voice rumbles above me. "*You* are not V'loryn."

"Yes, I am," I lie, remembering Amanda's warning.

He moves closer—a predator stalking his prey. His nails

extend into sharpened claws and he grasps my chin in a bruising grip. "If you were, you would know exactly what I am." I bite back a whimper as the deadly points dig into my flesh. His gaze holds mine as he speaks in a low and menacing voice. "Do you know what I am?"

His lips pull back in a feral snarl as his canines extend into deadly fangs.

Fear steals my breath and stops my heart. "Vampire," I barely manage. The monster of ancient Terran myth and legend standing before me. *Death*—the word echoes in my mind, but I dare not even breathe it aloud.

He cocks his head to the side. "Interesting. You are not the first to call me by this name. But you are wrong. I am A'kai. But you will call me Master. Now. Tell me what you are."

"I-"

"The truth, this time," he growls.

Panic tightens my chest as his glowing green eyes turn into feral obsidian orbs. I open my mouth to speak, but the words die in my throat.

"Very well, then," he says. "I will find the truth myself."

His gaze holds mine as blood rushes through my ears, drowning out all other sounds. Pressure grows in the back of my mind—a giant wave building behind a dam.

Without warning, the barrier crumbles, and I instantly feel him inside me. I want to scream as the full force of his consciousness invades and expands in my mind, but my body won't respond.

Searing pain rips through me as the sharp blade of his thoughts cut through mine, forcing my body and mind to bend to his will.

Through the connection, I understand that he is A'kai—a race spoken of in scared and hushed whispers. Perverse delight dances across the landscape of his dark and twisted mind as he tears through my consciousness and finds his answer.

"You are Terran," his voice echoes in my thoughts through the telepathic connection. *"Your kind are a delicacy to mine."*

I choke on a scream as he sinks his teeth deep into my neck and begins to drink of my blood. Rage wars with devastation as tears of despair roll down my cheeks.

Is this how I will die?

"No," he replies in my mind, having heard my thoughts. *"I will keep you for myself. Your blood is too valuable—restorative healing properties unlike anything my race has ever encountered before. I will keep you, and you will lead me to your home world and your people. With Terran blood, we will expand our Empire. Even the Mosaurans and the V'loryns will be unable to stand against us."*

Darkness closes in at the edge of my vision as he continues to drink of my blood. Closing my eyes, I fall away into the cold and beckoning void.

Days have turned into weeks and months. I dream in colors. The vivid oranges and red of a dawning sky fill my mind.

How long has it been since I've seen the sun?

Long enough the colors have begun to bleed together in my memories. Surely, they are too perfect and vibrant to have ever been real. Even so… these images are mine. I believed my thoughts were the only things that could never be taken from me, but I was wrong. With their telepathic abilities, nothing is safe from the A'kai; they can take anything that they want.

Every time Falen drinks my blood and invades my mind, he searches my memories—tearing through my consciousness for anything that might lead his people to my home world.

If they find it, I have no doubt they will conquer Terra and enslave our people. Their tech is far superior to ours. I can only pray they never find our planet.

Time has no meaning in space, certainly not inside a cage in a dark cargo hold. So, when a beam of light splits the darkness as the cargo bay doors slide open, I don't know if it's night or day on the ship. I only know one of the A'kai masters is returning with three of the girls he took earlier.

Despite knowing how this goes, my body involuntarily begins trembling as Falen opens the cage beside mine and throws Alana back inside. He leans in and runs his fingers through her long, blonde hair, lifting it to his nose before stepping back and closing the door to her cage. Her eyes swim with tears as she curls onto her side on the floor.

He turns to me, and I brace myself.

His green eyes glow brightly in the dark, casting just enough light I can make out his angular features, the sharp tips of his elvish ears, and the green tinge of his skin.

I press my fists into my lap to still their shaking, as I wait to hear the click of the lock opening. Squeezing my eyes shut, I try to go someplace else in my mind as I prepare to be taken.

He growls low, then I hear the sound of his bootsteps retreating. The soft whoosh of the doors sliding open, then closed, fills the silence, and I cautiously open my eyes.

His people must be sated. They drink from us in rotations, claiming our blood is the finest they've ever had. It is valuable to them because it also has the ability to heal any injury they sustain. I send another prayer to whomever may be listening that they never find our home world.

It's pitch black in here, and I know I cannot see, but still... I always try. I don't think I'll ever get used to the dark.

Muffled whimpers draw my attention to Alana's cage next to mine, and I scoot along on my knees to reach her.

The cages are too small for us to stand up, and my muscles ache in protest from being continually crouched down. I've been held prisoner for so long now, that I've conditioned myself to push through the pain. I reach out my hand to trace my fingers along the grated metal separating us and stop when I feel the warmth of her palm pressed against mine.

"Alana"— I lace my fingers with hers through the grating —"are you all right?"

A broken sob escapes her throat, and I squeeze her hands, wishing so much I could embrace her. We served on the same ship. Her and Harry—our engineer—were the only ones not in stasis sleep when we were taken. She blames herself for what happened, but after hearing her story, I know she and Harry fought bravely to save us from the Anguis that boarded our vessel.

We've been friends since flight school. She's like a sister to me. When she was brought aboard this ship, I could hardly believe it. When I woke up in a cage, I thought I'd never see any of my crew again.

"I keep hoping I'll wake up back on the ship"—Alana's voice quavers—"that I'll awaken to realize this was all just a terrible dream in the stasis pod. That we're on our way home to Terra." She pauses, her breathing less labored but shallow. "I saw him, Lara. I saw Harry. He's here on the ship."

My heart stops. "Are you sure?"

"Yes. It was only a glimpse, but I know it was him." Another sob escapes her. "He is such a gentle soul, Lara. I can't imagine what they are probably doing to him."

"At least we know he's alive," I whisper.

"He's my best friend," her voice quavers. "I should have fought harder. I should have—"

"Shhhh," I soothe as I grip her hand even tighter. "You did everything you could."

"You saw Harry?" Violet's voice cuts through the darkness. "I knew, from your description, that I was right. It *was* him, wasn't it?"

Violet was in the Terran space program, too—just like the rest of us, the last thing she remembers is going into stasis and waking up in a cage. It's the same story, over and over. The crazy thing is, somehow, we're still the same age as when we were taken, even though her ship disappeared twenty years before mine did.

Whoever abducted us must have kept us in stasis all that time, because as far as I can gather, each of us has only been awake less than a year.

"Yes," Alana replies. "That means there are more of us—more Terrans—being held on a different part of the ship, somewhere."

She's right. Every time I'm dragged from my cage and out into the rest of the ship, it seems like we travel through several different corridors. I don't know how large this vessel is, but I suspect it's probably much bigger than we first thought. The A'kai probably have dozens of slaves on board.

"We have to find a way out of here," I say, more to myself than to them.

"Where will we go?" Violet asks. "We don't even know where we are."

"Do you have a plan, Lara?" Mina's voice whispers in the darkness.

"We just have to get out of here," Elain's voice quavers. "Even if we die trying, it would be better than living like this."

"What if—" Violet starts, but stops as a piercing, high-pitched whine screeches through the ship.

The sound of metal grinding against metal is quickly

followed by a deafening boom rippling along the hull, and the ship rocks to one side, throwing us against our cages. I may not be familiar with alien tech, but I recognize the sound of an engine in distress.

"What was that?!"

Terrified but muffled whimpers sound in the darkness.

The doors whoosh open, and Falen races into the cargo bay. Red lights flash behind him in the hallway, and sirens blare in warning.

He flips a switch along the wall, and all the cage locks snap open. "Get out!" We're evacuating!"

"What's going on?" I ask, unable to hide the panic in my voice.

"We're being pulled through a worm hole," he barks. "It's tearing apart the ship."

Before I can think to ask anything else, a voice drones over the speakers. "Five minutes until hull integrity failure."

"Move!" he snarls. "We have to go!"

We scramble from our cages and follow after Falen, racing down the corridor. He's so fast, we can barely keep up. I hold Alana's hand tightly, glancing back at her, the red flashing lights turning her golden hair pink as we run. A'kai soldiers hurry past us, terror easily read in their otherwise monstrous features.

"Evacuate the Terrans!" the Captain roars.

Falen glances over his shoulder, his eyes blazing with anger. "Hurry up!"

When we finally catch up to him, he continues down the hallway, and we rush after him. Rounding a corner, we enter into a massive room lined with what I can only guess are escape pods. They look like they should only fit one person, but I watch as A'kai soldiers file into them in pairs.

"I need one soldier for every Terran," Falen yells.

Several of the A'kai snap their heads in our direction, and I note how eagerly many of them move toward us.

Alana hugs me tightly to her. "No," she whimpers. Warm tears spill from her cheeks and onto my shoulders. "I don't want to leave you."

I draw in a shaking breath, holding back tears and running a hand over her hair. "I don't either—"

My words are cut short as an arm snakes around my waist and jerks me away.

Alana cries out as another soldier grips her forearm and drags her to a pod.

I kick out at Falen, fighting against his hold.

Screams and terror-filled shouts pierce the chaos as soldiers drag each of us to the pods. No one in their right mind wants to be alone with the A'kai. Not after what happened to Sarah. She died after losing too much blood because one of the A'kai got carried away as he drank from her.

That's why the Captain began rotating us out for his men, hoping to avoid them draining us to the point of death.

Falen pulls me into a pod and straps me to one of two seats. "If you want to live, you'll be quiet."

I bite my lip, struggling to hold back a whimper as he tightens the harness. The straps dig into my flesh so tightly it's a wonder it doesn't cut through my skin.

Falen straps into the chair beside me. I watch as he taps a series of symbols on the screen, powering up the display console. A green light flashes in the corner, and with a loud rush of air, the pod violently ejects, catapulting away from the ship.

I watch several others fly past, the massive A'kai vessel growing smaller in the viewscreen with each passing moment, as we tumble away in the dark void of space.

A blinding yellow-orange flash fills the viewscreen as the A'kai ship explodes in a brilliant display of light.

I grit my teeth, waiting for the shock wave to hit us.

Falen shouts, "Hold on!"

The wave crashes against the hull, and the pod shudders turbulently, sending us spiraling through the darkness.

Bile rises in my throat as fear twists deep inside me.

Alarms blare through the speakers as red lights flash in warning. Falen punches several controls on the panel then slams his fist down on the screen, snarling in frustration.

A gray-blue planet appears in the distance, covered in clouds.

The hull creeks and groans as the pod begins to shudder. A wall of flame flares brightly outside the viewscreen, signaling the beginning of our descent into the upper atmosphere. The computer flashes images of the escape vessel, and from the picture, I surmise it's a warning the hull is so damaged we may not survive entry.

The interior heats to near-boiling temperatures, and I send a silent prayer to whomever may be listening that we don't burn up before we reach the planet's surface.

I focus on the screen as an icy landscape races toward us. The hull scrapes the top of a snow-covered peak, and I squeeze my eyes shut, bracing for impact.

The entire structure shakes violently as we crash through a dense forest of trees, rushing toward the valley below. A deafening boom explodes throughout the cabin.

My harness tears, and I pitch forward, slamming against the wall upon impact. My vision goes dark.

CHAPTER 2

MARKUS

I stand on the great wall, looking out upon the vast expanse of ice and the snow-covered forest. The red needle-like leaves cast an orange-red glow on the snow around them, orange sunlight spilling through their branches. The air is crisp. A cold breeze whips around my wings and through my short, dark hair. I look up at the pale blue sky, watching the storm clouds gather in the distance.

It has been five cycles my warriors and I have been stranded here on this cursed planet. I would give anything to see the lavender skies of my home world—Mosaura—once more.

My gaze shifts to the clear ice blocks beneath me, that comprise our wall, and I study my reflection. Before we crashed, I used to buff my silver scales daily into a fine sheen, hoping to attract a female and entice her to fight me in the mating battle.

Females tend to prefer the more brightly colored males

and I used to lament that the only coloring I had, that was not dull, was the green accents of my cheeks and brow.

My violet eyes reflect back at me, reminding me of my father, and I wonder if my family holds out hope I am alive. Perhaps, they already count me among the dead, mourning me as they have mourned my brother ever since the Creator took him from us. Each night, I offer a prayer to the Creator they do not, that we will somehow be rescued and returned to our planet and our people.

Until that day comes, however, we are warriors of Mosaura and we will hold this territory in the name of the Mosauran Empire.

Movement catches my eye in the distance, and I glance up to see Rokan flying overhead. His silver-white scales catching the sunlight, nearly blinding me with their brightness.

He lands beside me. His reflective green eyes meet mine and he bows low. "Commander, I have found no evidence of any further attempts to breach our wall."

"Excellent, Rokan."

"The V'loryns are still working futilely on their ship and, now, they are even working with the Aerilons."

A low growl rumbles my chest. Two enemies working together is never good. "You are certain the Aerilons are helping them?"

"Yes."

I draw in a deep breath as I consider the implications. The Aerilons are capable of flight, like our people. If the V'loryns have allied with them, this could give them an advantage they would otherwise not have had.

"What of the Lycaons and the A'kai?"

"The Lycaons are savages," he snarls. "They remain mostly in their shifted forms, hunting in the forests like the four-legged beasts they are." He pauses. "And the A'kai have fortified their defenses. It seems they've managed to repair the shields of their ship. It surrounds their complex, making it impenetrable."

I curl my hands into fists, in frustration. This is troubling news on all sides. It is one thing to be stranded on an unknown planet but another to be surrounded by one's enemies. I wish they had crashed on the opposite side of the planet instead of so close to us. I suppose it could not be helped since we were all pulled through that star-cursed wormhole together.

"Commander Markus, what are your orders?" Rokan asks, pulling me back from my thoughts.

I meet his green gaze evenly. "We are warriors of Mosaura. We will defend this territory in the name of the Empire. No one shall take from us that which is ours."

He crosses his arm over his body and thumps his fist to his chest. "We are warriors of Mosaura," he repeats. "We will hold these lands in the name of the Empire."

I glance over my shoulder at my warriors down below. Already, they are gathering around the fire as the sun sets low on the horizon.

"Will you join us for evening meal, Commander?"

I dip my chin. "When I am done with my watch."

He bows, then flies down to the courtyard as I survey all we have built, with pride.

Our great ice wall stands proudly before the towering mountain behind it, protecting our crashed ship, partially buried in the rock face. Our vessel may never fly again, but our engineers have found ways to tap into its power to run everything inside our territory.

We have carved out homes in the cliff walls and excavated an interior network of tunnels—living as our ancestors once did in caves on Mosaura.

There are fifteen of us, total. Rokan is one of our engineers. He works tirelessly on our wrecked vessel, trying to repair communications. It has been many cycles, but he refuses to give up. All of us do. The expectation of rescue has never wavered in our minds.

The Empire is vast, and our technology superior to many of the other races. There is always the possibility our people will find us, and I have not yet given up hope.

As I peer out over the snow-covered forest, I remember my father's sage words: *The Creator of all things set our fate into motion long before we were born. We must trust him to direct our steps upon the path he has laid out before us.*

He told me this shortly after the death of my brother. I suppose it is how he reconciles, in his heart, the terrible loss that devastated our family.

A bright flash of light draws my attention. I look to the sky, and my mouth drifts open as a trail of fire blazes across the icy landscape. It is not uncommon for meteorite debris to penetrate the atmosphere, but this is larger than any I have seen before.

I observe as several others join it, the loud boom as they enter the planet's atmosphere reverberating loudly throughout the forest. Squinting, I note they are vessels— escape pods of some sort—but I cannot make out their design from this far away.

Rokan joins me on the wall, followed by several of my warriors. "What are they?" he asks.

"Escape pods, but I do not know what kind. We must investigate."

A strange warmth fills my chest as I watch them fall. Something about these objects resonates deep in my soul. Tracking their descent, I cannot ignore the pull I feel toward them, and I must know why.

I have always trusted my intuition. It has never failed me before; I will not ignore it now.

I look to my warriors. "I will go into the forest and investigate these vessels."

"Send me, Commander," Rokan says. "I will go in your stead."

It is a point of pride I never ask of my warriors anything I, myself, would not do. We each take turns keeping watch in various outposts deep in the forest. It is imperative that we monitor the territory that separates us from our enemies, ensuring they do not amass their forces and prepare to invade and try to take what we have. "No, it is my rotation. Stay here. Guard the wall. I will report back what I find."

"I am uncertain," Healer Siran's voice draws my attention, "but those craft appeared A'kai, in design."

I study Siran. The purple scales of his cheeks and brow stand out in sharp contrast to his dark-gray scales. His silver eyes meet mine, and I recognize the worry etched in his features. He is right. Their dart-like appearance does remind me of the A'kai escape pods, but there are other races that use a similar design. "From this far away, it is hard to tell," I agree. "That is why it is best only one of us goes. We cannot leave our territory unprotected."

"Does it have to be you?" he asks, in a calm challenge. He is the only one who would speak to me in this way. We trained together as warriors. He is my friend, and I know he means no disrespect. Rather, he is worried. "You should send one of us."

I tip up my chin. "A Commander never neglects his duty"—I scan the faces of my warriors—"I will leave immediately."

Each of my warriors crosses an arm over their chests and thumps their fists to their hearts as they bow low.

Rokan steps forward. "Are you certain you do not wish to delay?" He lifts his gaze to the sky and the dark clouds gathering overhead. "The storm will be upon us soon."

In his eyes, I recognize his concern. There are predators on this world that are deadly and formidable. Most of them are nocturnal and hunt the forests and the ice plains at night.

With a slight clench of my jaw, I survey the woods again.

I must know what fell from the sky this night. I will not be at peace until I have an answer.

"I am certain. I will return in seven days—at the end of my rotation." I gesture to my wristband. "I will attempt to maintain contact as often as I can."

Aside from the zorolian-like layer of rock beneath the forest floor that interferes with our communications equipment, this planet is known for its violent and unpredictable storms. They follow no patterns that we are familiar with or have ever encountered before on different worlds across the Empire. These two factors make communications nearly impossible to maintain despite how many signal towers we have placed along the mountain range.

As I think again on the objects that fell from the sky, my conviction to discover what they are only deepens. They are calling to me, and I cannot push aside this feeling there is something significant about them.

CHAPTER 3

LARA

The acrid smell of smoke fills my nostrils, and I burst into consciousness. Fire fills my vision and I observe in horror as flames lick across the panel before me. Falen's head hangs down on his chest, his entire body limp and slumped forward in his chair.

Obsidian blood drips from his scalp down his front, pooling on the floor beneath him. Lights buzz and flicker overhead as fire travels up the damaged panels. Thick smoke and the heavy scent of burning metal fills the cabin as it melts the wiring.

Panic overwhelms my senses as the flames grow larger. I move to the hatch, grasping the handle firmly with both hands, trying to lift it up. Sharp pain stabs at my side and I gasp, banding my arm around my torso.

I don't know how badly I'm hurt, and I don't have time to assess my injuries now. I just need to get out of here before this entire pod burns up.

Gritting my teeth, I try the handle again. A sharp hiss of

air escapes when the hatch door cracks open. Metal screeches against metal as it meets resistance. I brace myself against the cabin wall and push on it as hard as I can.

After a moment, it gives way. I tumble forward, halfway out the door. Icy wind whips around me. I draw in a deep breath, frigid air burning my lungs with each inhalation. It's dark outside, but the light of twin moons overhead casts just enough illumination I can clearly see the snow-covered forest surrounding us.

I glance back at the path of broken trees left behind from our descent.

I'm lucky I survived.

I turn toward Falen, still unconscious in his seat as the fire continues to fill the cabin around him.

Before now, I always thought I was the kind of person who could never abandon another to death when I could help. But after all the terrible things he and the other A'kai did to my people, it's not even a question. I'm leaving him to burn.

I grip the side of the door to pull myself through, getting only halfway out when a strong hand wraps around my ankle, jerking me back. A low growl rumbles behind me, and the hair on the back of my neck rises as panic stills my heart.

"Did you think you would leave me here to die?" he snarls.

Without looking, I kick back with my free leg and hit something solid, igniting Falen's feral roar of anger.

He drags me into his arms, and I fight against his hold, kicking and screaming as he carries me out the door as if I weigh nothing. I choke on a cry when he wraps his hand around my throat in a vise-like grip, constricting the air from my lungs. I beat my fists against his chest, the edges of my vision beginning to go dark.

"Be still!" he growls. "I must feed so I may heal."

I open my mouth in a silent scream as the full force of his consciousness invades and expands in my mind. Searing pain rips through my skull, the sharp blade of his thoughts cutting through mine, forcing them into submission as he asserts his will.

I'm drowning in darkness, the crushing weight of his consciousness bearing down upon my own. Terror fills me, and I struggle to break free only to feel the unyielding brutality of his command over my body.

The razor-sharp lash of his thoughts whips at my mind, and I collapse before it.

This is why the A'kai are so feared. As I stare at the cruel lines of his face, his glowing, green eyes turn into obsidian orbs.

His fangs extend into sharpened points, and a tear slips down my cheek as I recognize the death that will claim me.

Using the last of my strength, I struggle against him, but it's no use. The A'kai are strong, and I can do nothing to stop him from leaning down to scent me, grazing his teeth along the curve of my neck. Goosebumps prickle my flesh when I feel something warm and wet drag across my skin, directly over my pulsing artery.

His dark desire floods my mind, and I choke on a scream when he sinks his teeth deep into my neck. The heavy scent of iron fills the air so thick I can taste it. The sick pull against my skin is agonizing torture as he drinks of my blood.

My pulse pounds in my ears, and I lay helpless beneath him. His hands clamp down on my arms in a bruising grip, and I'm unable to move, his consciousness holding mine prisoner.

Paralyzed under the crushing weight of his control, tears of despair and anger roll down my cheeks.

I think of Alana, Harry, and all the others, worried about where they are and if they made it. I think of my parents and how sad they'll be never knowing what happened to their daughter. A broken sob escapes me. I wish I could have seen home one more time.

Movement in the corner of my eye catches my attention, and I watch, stunned, as a blur of silver rushes toward us, slamming into Falen and knocking him away from me.

Lighting fast, Falen spins on his attacker. I'm so weak, I can barely focus, struggling to make out what's happening. A bellowing roar fills the air as the creature claws and tears into the A'kai's flesh.

Falen cries out, then goes silent. I turn onto my side as his attacker rushes forward, dropping to his knees before me.

Reflective, violet eyes stare down at me intently, vertically slit pupils contracting, then expanding, examining my form.

I barely manage to lift my arm, trying to shield myself. "Please" I whisper. "Don't hurt me."

"I am Commander Markus of the Mosauran Empire and the Great House of Sarodan. I will not harm you. I swear it to the Creator."

Mosauran.

I've heard others mention his people. Despite his words, I cannot help but be afraid when I notice the two rows of sharp fangs when he speaks. His species is among the most feared in the quadrant. They are known as a race of warriors. Even the A'kai speak of them in hushed tones and whispers.

He's covered in smooth, silver scales that shimmer softly beneath the moonlight. Deep-silver-gray wings are tucked close to his back. His entire body is layers of thick, corded muscle. It is easy to see from his build that this man is a warrior. His fingers are tipped with lethal black claws that retract as soon as he notices my gaze upon them.

He has accented highlights of green across the sharp ridges of his cheeks and brows. A bony, ridge starts at the top of his forehead and spreads out across his skull in a *V*, disappearing into short-cropped, obsidian hair. With an aristo-cratic nose and a masculine, square jaw, he is fierce and beautiful all at once as he stares down at me.

There's a kindness reflected behind his violet eyes, and despite all I've been through, my instincts urge me to trust him. But, as I think on my first impression of the A'kai, I learned long ago that beauty can mask monsters.

"Please," I whisper again. "Don't hurt me."

CHAPTER 4

MARKUS

Luminous, gray-blue eyes, the color of starlight, stare up into mine.

Ashaya.

The word moves through me; the awareness that I am irrevocably hers resonating deep in my soul. She is now as much a part of me as the heart beating solidly within my chest. I am bound to her by celestial fate. I have found the one who makes me whole.

My heart clenches as she begs me not to hurt her. I take her in, and can hardly believe my fated one is V'loryn. I've never heard of any of my kind finding their mate outside of our species. That her race is a blood enemy of mine makes it all the more astonishing. And yet, I find her beautiful, despite this fact.

She is smaller than most V'loryns, and her eyes are a lovely shade of blue instead of the normal glowing green typical of her kind.

Her ears are rounded instead of pointed at the top, and I

gasp as I notice the cut on her scalp seeps red blood instead of black.

Rage fills me as I study the two puncture wounds along her neck from the A'kai and the many dark bruise marks along her otherwise-pale skin. Fierce protectiveness rushes through me. "I swear to the Creator I will not harm you. You are safe now. I will protect you."

She takes my hand and squeezes it gently. "Thank you," she barely manages before her head tips back, falling unconscious.

I reach down and tap my wristband communicator, frowning when I realize I have no signal.

Fear washes over me, and I gather her in my arms, close to my chest, surprised by how slight is her weight. She is injured and weak. I must get her back to our mountain and Healer Siran.

Spreading my wings out to my sides, I lift into the air. Storm clouds unfurl across the sky, blocking the light of the twin moons and the stars above. Although my people possess superior night vision, the heavy snowfall raining down from above makes it difficult to navigate through the blizzard. The mountain range, normally so easily visible in the distance, is now hidden from me.

My eyes rise once more, searching for the star that will guide my path, but see nothing but dark clouds.

The wind picks up, clawing at my form and trying to rip my Ashaya from my arms. I wrap them even tighter around her smaller frame. I have no choice but to take her to the outpost. There is an emergency med kit there that I need in order to treat her.

Through the whirling flakes, I glance down at the forest below—the trees and the ground are blanketed in white. I swoop down low over the tree line, toward the edge of the woods in the valley between two great mountains.

Carefully, I land and make my way to the shelter pod. It is cloaked and not visible from outside, but I know exactly where it is. I have been here many times. When we first crashed on this planet, we took three of these from our ship and deployed them to various places throughout the forest as outposts to guard and patrol our territory.

Shifting so I am holding my Ashaya in one arm, I grab a felled branch, full of leaves, with another and pull it behind us to cover our tracks. They should be covered shortly by the falling snow, but I will not risk being discovered. Not when this outpost is so close to the territories held by our enemies.

When I reach the door, I tap the control, and it slides open immediately. Flaring my nostrils, I inhale deeply, glad when I note no scent, save that of my own warriors, lingers in this place. It has not been discovered nor used by any others.

I sweep the room, and everything appears to be just as it should be; nothing out of place. I carry her over to the bed in the corner, setting her gently down atop the white furs covering it.

I am glad I made as many of these as I did from my kills. They are much softer and warmer than the bedding that originally came with this pod. I pull the emergency med kit from the table beside the bed and search the bag for the tissue regenerating gel.

It doesn't take long to find it, but as I assess her unconscious form, I worry about using it. Meant for use in the heat of battle, it reknits torn tissue quickly, but the process is quite painful.

Her people are very strong, however. More so than mine, in some ways. They are faster, and their strength is equal to our own. As I study her face, my mind still struggles with the fact that my Ashaya is V'loryn.

I cup her cheek, marveling at her petal-soft skin against

my scaled palm. I study her gently arched brows, her delicate nose and her soft, perfect lips. Her features are elegant and beautiful, instead of the hardened, fierce appearance of a female Mosauran.

I lift a lock of her long, brown hair, the silken strands soft as they slip through my fingers.

My protective instincts flare as I turn my attention again to the tops of her rounded ears, which should be pointed. She lacks the slight cranial ridges of her people, and she is much smaller than their typical females. Anger floods my veins as I think on all the terrible things she must have endured to have changed her so drastically.

She jerks awake, emitting a panicked cry. She immediately scrambles away on the bed, her back hitting the wall of the shelter. Her chest rises and falls rapidly.

"Leave me alone!"

My nose wrinkles at the acrid scent of her fear, and I move back, holding my hands out to her in a placating gesture. "I vow I will not harm you."

"Then, why are you partially undressed?"

I glance downward. Only my upper half is exposed. Most times, especially when guarding the outpost, I wear nothing. Clothing does not survive the shift into *draken* form. But it appears her kind may be like the V'loryns, who detest nudity. I meet her eyes evenly. "I would never force myself upon you. I swear it to the Creator."

Her wild gaze sweeps the room. "Where is the A'kai?"

"Dead."

She regards me warily. "I've heard of your people. The masters said Mosaurans put all slavers to death."

"We do."

It concerns me to hear her speak of my kind as though she is unfamiliar with us. Our races have been enemies for thousands of cycles. I look up at the injury to her scalp, still seeping blood.

Stars, she must have hit her head much harder than I thought.

Her shoulders visibly relax.

"My kind detest the slavers," I add. "Just as your people— the V'loryns—do. I vow you are safe. I would never harm you. What is your name?"

CHAPTER 5

LARA

The fact his kind hates slavery makes me believe I can tell him the truth. I have to, if I want his help finding my friends.

"My name is Lara Martin."

"Lara Martin," he repeats to himself. His brow furrows deeply as he lifts his violet eyes to me. "Martin is the name of your family's Great House?"

"No, I—" Drawing in a deep breath, I steal myself for what I'm about to say next. "I'm not V'loryn."

He cocks his head to the side. "Then, what are you?"

"Terran."

"I have never heard of your race before."

"That's because my people have never left our planetary system."

His mouth drifts open. "Then, how did you end up with the A'kai?"

"The last thing I remember, I was on my way home from Mars." He blinks in confusion. "It's a planet close to my home world—in our same planetary system. I went into stasis sleep, along with the rest of my crew, for the journey. The next thing I knew, I woke up in a cage on an Anguis slave ship. They sold me to the A'kai.

"There were at least twenty of us on the ship with the A'kai; probably more. Their ship was large." I pause. "Most people think we're V'loryn, but the A'kai somehow know we are not. They purposely bought us for our blood. They were taking us back to their home world."

I continue. "They searched our minds for Terra's location, but none of us know it because we've never traveled outside of our own system before. I'm a navigator and even I have no idea how to find Terra."

His jaw clenches as he listens to me, and his eyes shine with pity. "I am sorry, Lara. I cannot imagine how hard it must have been for you."

A stray tear escapes my lashes, but I quickly brush it away. "Thank you," I whisper.

I inspect our shelter. It isn't very big, but it would comfortably fit four people. It reminds me a bit of a yurt but with some luxury items, like the computer panel in the wall beside us.

I'm on a bed piled high with soft, white furs, and across the way is a gray sofa. The entire space is rather sparse, but at least it's warm. "Where are we? Is this your home?"

A smile tilts his lips. "No. I have brought you to a shelter at the edge of the forest. There is a storm outside." He turns and taps a symbol on the nearby panel.

The walls shimmer and turn transparent, allowing me to see the outside as if I were sitting in the middle of the forest with no walls around or ceiling above us.

My jaw drops. The woods and the ground are blanketed in a thick layer of white as a blizzard rages outside. I reach out, wondering if I can touch anything. When my hand hits the wall, I snap my head back to Markus. "How are you doing this?"

"This is a shelter pod. It is cloaked; not visible from the outside. The transparent walls from in here make it easily defendable. No enemies can sneak up on you while you're inside without you being able to see them." He gestures to a door across the way. "There is a cleansing room on the other side, complete with an ion shower."

He studies me a moment. "Do you remember how you ended up here? On this planet?"

"The A'kai ship was damaged when it was pulled into a wormhole. We had to evacuate. They split all of us up. One A'kai for each of my people went into the escape pods." I think on the others. "Have you seen anyone else like me?"

"No," he replies, and my heart sinks.

He reaches for a bag in a compartment next to the bed. "This is an emergency med kit." He gestures to the satchel. "We must apply the healing gel for your injuries."

"Healing gel?"

He produces a small tube with writing I cannot understand and holds it out to me. "This will sting when it is applied, but you must refrain from touching it while it reknits your tissue."

The thought of more pain makes me cringe inwardly, but I force myself to be brave. This man may appear formidable, but if he'd wanted to hurt me, he could have already done so over a dozen times. So far, he's been nothing but kind to me, and I'm inclined to trust him.

"All right."

I watch as he squeezes the thick, clear gel onto his fingers. He lifts his hand to my head, rubs the salve over the injury on my scalp, and applies it to the two puncture wounds on my neck. Not even a minute after it's applied, intense pain sears like fire burning across my skin.

Instinctively, I reach up to wipe it off, but lightning fast he grips my wrists, pulling them away. I struggle against his hold as he pulls me into his chest, immobilizing me. Dark memories fill my mind of the A'kai cutting deep into my flesh when they marked my back.

"You must allow it to work," he grits through his teeth.

"It burns!" I cry out, desperate to wipe it away. Anything to end this torment, but he won't release me. "Let me go!"

"I cannot," he grinds out.

After what feels like an eternity, the burning subsides, and he releases his grip. My entire body is trembling as I reach up to touch my scalp and then the space where the two puncture wounds were on my neck. I'm surprised when I feel smoothly closed skin in its place.

His violet eyes meet mine. "Are you all right?"

"I am now. But... why did that hurt so much?"

"It is part of an emergency kit, meant to be used in the midst of battle. It must repair tissue rapidly," he says, as if that explains everything.

Glancing out at the snowstorm, my thoughts turn again to my friends. "My people... the ones who came down on the other escape pods... they're probably still out there."

He surveys the woods and the heavy snow falling outside. "We should remain here until the storm has passed. After that, we can begin searching for your people." He pauses. "I should send a signal to mine and warn them of the A'kai."

He turns to the control panel and taps a few strange symbols. The screen lights up, but nothing happens. He frowns as he presses another series of controls before grumbling low in frustration. He turns to me. "The storm is blocking my signal. I will try again, once it passes."

He looks me over, and I instinctively shrink away.

As though sensing my discomfort, he quickly averts his

gaze. "Forgive me, Lara. It is just… you appear so much like a V'loryn and, yet… also so different."

"I've never seen a V'loryn before."

"How long ago were you taken?"

"I—I don't know." Tears sting my eyes, but I blink them back. "For me, it feels as though I've only been away for six months at most. But… I could have been asleep for years."

Decades, even.

He cocks his head to the side. "What do you mean?"

"I met another Terran on one of the stations, before I was sold to the A'kai. I recognized her name. She'd been missing for at least ten years, and yet… she appeared as though she hadn't aged a day. I think they kept us in stasis up until a few months ago. I don't know how long I was asleep."

A deep ache settles in my chest. "My entire family could already be dead by now, for all I know."

His expression is full of pity. "I am sorry, Lara. Truly. I know what it is to be so far from home. It has been many cycles since I have seen my home world—Mosaura."

I draw in a collecting breath, pushing down my sadness, and change the subject. "If this isn't your home world, why are you here?"

"My warriors and I have been stranded here for the past five cycles. As were the others we were fighting. Our ships were pulled into a wormhole, and we crashed on this planet when we came out the other side."

"What others?"

"There are V'loryns, Aerilons, Lycaons and A'kai here.

"There were several escape pods that launched from the A'kai ship. Did you see any of them?"

"I saw them as they fell from the sky," he says. "It is why I left our territory to investigate."

My thoughts shift to the other races he named. "The other species you mentioned… the ones who crashed here, too. Do you think they would harm my people, if they found them?"

"The A'kai would. The rest... I do not believe so, but many of them are enemies of the Empire. As such, my people have tried to minimize our interactions with them. And now we are all stranded here on this planet, we have each taken up separate territories, defending them against invasion."

My eyes widen as I think on my friends. "Please, Markus," I beg. "Will you help me find my people?"

He dips his chin. "Yes. When we do, we will bring them back to our territory where they will be safe." He turns his focus to the outside. "But, we must wait until the storm completely clears."

He seems genuinely kind. Is this too good to be true?

After all the pain I've suffered at the hands of others in this part of the universe, I can hardly believe I've come across someone not only willing to help me, but to help my friends, as well.

But, as I observe his form, and the thick cords of muscle wrapping around his arms and legs, his broad shoulders and hard planes of muscles, I realize he could easily overpower me, if he wished.

As though reading my thoughts, he drops to one knee before me and bows his head. When he lifts his face, his violet eyes meet mine evenly. "I will never harm you, Lara. I will protect you, and I will help you find your people. I swear it to the Creator."

Emotions lodge in my throat at the sincerity of his words, but I somehow manage to speak around them. "Thank you."

CHAPTER 6

MARKUS

S he lifts her eyes up to the sky and the snow falling thickly overhead. "How long do you think this will last?"

"Some storms pass through rather quickly, but it is not unusual for them to last many days."

Her expression fills with worry, and I realize I probably should not have said this. Her people are still out there.

"Because of the mountains, there are many caves that offer shelter," I offer, wishing I could give her more than just words of hope.

If I could, I'd be out there searching for her people even now. Not just for her sake, but for them. The A'kai are ruthless and cruel. Bile rises in the back of my throat as I think on how they treat their slaves.

So many that we rescued were irrevocably damaged by the *R'ugol*—the forced link that violates the mind of their victims. The A'kai are monsters.

I recall her words and how she mentioned the A'kai

searched her mind for the location of her home world. My Ashaya is much stronger than she seems to have endured such a terrible thing.

Even my own people—known for their strength—have had their minds broken by the R'ugol.

My hands curl into fists at my side. I wish I could kill all those who ever touched her against her will. "I vow that we will search for your people, Lara. As soon as the storm clears, we will do all that we can to find them."

She nods, but the concern is easily read in her features. I wonder, now, how I could ever have mistaken her for a V'loryn. Their faces are impassive masks; their people suppress their emotions.

"Are you hungry? Thirsty?"

"Both, actually."

I turn to the stasis unit and retrieve some of the dried meat I stored from my last kill. It is much better than emergency protein bars. I hand her a few strips. She frowns as she studies it.

"What is this?"

"Dried meat." I tip my head up with pride, glad I can provide for my Ashaya. "It is from my kill, last time I was here."

She lifts a strip to her nose and sniffs. "It smells good." She takes a bite, and a low hum escapes her throat. "This tastes wonderful."

I puff my chest out with pride. "Have as much as you like. There is plenty."

A horrible thought moves through me as I observe her flat, white teeth and her blunt nails. I lean in, studying her intently.

"What's wrong?" she asks.

"Are you... fully matured?"

"What?" she asks, disbelief lacing her tone. "What kind of question is that?"

"You have no fangs or claws… and you are rather small."

She blinks at me. "Yes, I'm fully matured. My people *don't* have fangs or claws. And I'm average height for my species."

My brows shoot up to my forehead. She must hail from a very temperate planet indeed.

How have her people managed to survive as a species with no natural defenses?

As my gaze travels over her, I worry about our future fledglings. I only hope they take more after their Mosauran heritage in this regard. Then again, we may not even be capable of creating life with our joining. After all, we are two different species.

And… she has not yet even agreed to become my mate. She may not even want me.

I push my dark thoughts aside as I regard her. For one so small, I am glad she at least has a healthy appetite. It is a male's greatest point of pride to be able to provide for his mate.

"This reminds me of the jerky my sister and I used to eat when we were kids." A faint smile crests her lips.

"How many siblings do you have?"

Sadness flits across her expression. "Just my older sister, but she died a few years ago in a transport accident."

"My heart grieves with yours," I offer the Mosauran shared words of mourning.

"Thank you," she murmurs. "What about you? Do you have any brothers or sisters?"

I close my eyes briefly against the pain. "I had a brother. He died a few years ago in a border skirmish with the Aerilons."

"I'm sorry for your loss."

Sadness tightens my chest. "Thank you."

"The Aerilons... I've heard of them. They have wings also, right?"

"Yes."

"And... your people are at war with them?"

"Not quite. There is a long and bloody history between us, but currently, we have a treaty of non-aggression. But there are still battles fought along our borders, despite this."

She reaches across and places her hand atop mine, squeezing it gently as her blue eyes stare deep into my own. "I'm sorry you lost your brother. It's a terrible thing to lose your sibling."

I nod, and then study her a moment. "Do you have any other family? A mate?"

I wait, anxious for her to answer, praying she says there is no male waiting for her to return.

"No, I don't."

I want to roar my happiness to the stars she is not already claimed by another.

"I mean... I dated," she adds, "but it never really turned into anything, you know."

I do not know.

"What is 'dated'?"

"It's dating," she corrects. "It's basically where you spend time with someone so you can decide if you want to be with them forever or not."

I tilt my head to the side to regard her. "This is how you choose a mate?"

"Yes."

"Is there a battle involved?"

Her head jerks back. "Battle? What do you mean?"

"My people have a mating battle—the *shav-rhokan*. It is how we choose a mate."

Her jaw drops. "What?"

48

"Do Terran females not challenge males to fight to determine if they will be a worthy mate?"

"Uh… no."

"Then, how does a Terran female choose her partner? How does she know if a male will give her strong fledglings, if she doesn't know he can defeat her in battle?"

A surprised laugh escapes her, but I do not understand what it is about my statement she finds funny. Perhaps something is not translating correctly between us. I study her intently and her face falls.

"Wait… you're serious?"

I nod.

"Explain this… mating battle to me."

"When a female is interested in taking a mate—usually during her mating heat—she will challenge a group of males, or sometimes one male, by announcing 'shav-rhokan.' If the males are interested in becoming her mate, they will fight her. Whichever male defeats her, then he gives her his mark by biting her neck, and she accepts him into her body, and they become a mated pair. He shares his life essence with her, joining their hearts and their souls as one."

Her eyes widen, but she says nothing.

"Because the shav-rhokan usually happens during the mating heat, an egg often follows shortly after. It is then the male's job to guard the nest. That is why the mating battle is so important. A female must be able to trust a male is strong enough to guard their egg and protect their future offspring."

"Egg?" she asks, disbelief lacing her tone. "Did you say 'egg'?"

"Yes. Do your people not lay eggs?"

"Umm… no. No, we don't."

"Then, how do you have young?"

"We carry them inside us until they're born."

My jaw drops. "That sounds… painful."

"So does laying an egg," she offers. I suppose she is right. I have heard females complain of the discomfort of laying an egg.

I analyze her smaller figure and wonder how her people survive such a birthing process. I've heard the Aerilons and V'loryns have their young in this way, but their females are also larger than she is.

If she accepts me as her mate, I am not sure it would be wise for us to have any fledglings. I do not believe the Creator would have gifted us the fated bond unless we were compatible in this way, but I do not want any harm to come to her. I would not want to risk her life like this.

When she is finished eating, I pull out a changing of clothes from the emergency pack and gesture to the bed. "You may change into these." I hand them to her. "Then, you may lie down to rest."

She stills. "Are you… going to sleep there, too?" I do not miss the slight tremor of her hands as she fists them into her lap to still their shaking.

Anger flares inside me at the abuse she must have withstood to be so afraid I might try to take advantage of her. I move quickly to reassure her I would never harm her in any way. "No. I will sleep on the sofa."

Her shoulders visibly relax. "Thank you."

I dip my chin.

"Will you turn around while I change?"

I frown. My people think nothing of nudity, but it seems hers do. I was right. They *are* similar to the V'loryns in this way. I turn my back as she changes. A hiss of pain escapes her lips, and I straighten. "Are you all right?"

"Just some muscle pain. That's all." I hear a tearing of fabric a moment later but remain silent. If she needs any help, I hope she trusts me enough to ask.

When she is finished, she calls out. "You can turn back around now."

The clothing is quite large on her smaller form. The pants are so big she has tied them to her waist with a strip of fabric torn from her slave gown.

The bottom hem of the emergency shirt comes to her mid-thigh, and the arms are so long, she rolls them up, bunching the fabric over her forearms to expose her hands.

When we return to my people, we will have to figure out some clothing for her.

I watch as she rearranges the many furs on the bed as if building a nest.

I wonder if she is approaching her mating heat.

Mosauran females build nests during this time.

I only pray this is not the case with my Ashaya. It is obvious she has been through much. If her heat cycle comes, I will have to leave her, because it could trigger my own, and I know she is probably not ready for a mating. It may be a long time before she is. There is also the possibility she may not wish to take me as her mate anyway.

"Are you nesting?" I must know. If she is, I will have to leave her. Immediately.

"Nesting?"

"Yes. Are you entering your heat cycle?"

She blinks. "My people don't have a heat cycle." She glances down at the furs and the pillows all around her. "I was just rearranging things, and I was going to make you a bed on the sofa, as well."

A smile crests my lips.

She is preparing a bed for me?

Has any male ever been so blessed with such a thoughtful mate? Most females would never even think of their mate's comfort in this way.

I do not want to take anything from her, however. Her

comfort is far more important than mine. "I do not need any pillows or furs. I am fine sleeping on the couch as I am."

She frowns. "Are you sure?"

"Yes."

After she settles beneath the furs, I lie down on the sofa. With a heavy sigh, I watch the storm through the transparent walls.

The A'kai are very intelligent and skilled hunters. This makes them dangerous. I am glad we are sheltered in this pod. It will be easy to watch for them while remaining concealed here.

Rage twists deep inside me as I think on the one who tried to kill her. My warriors and I will hunt down and kill every one of the A'kai slavers that crashed on this planet, just to be certain she and her people are safe. I swear it to the Creator.

CHAPTER 7

MARKUS

She curls onto her side beneath the blanket of furs. "Please," she whispers under her breath. "Don't betray me."

My heart clenches. She spoke so low, I do not believe her words were meant to be overheard. I want only to reassure and comfort her, but I know that my actions will do this more effectively than anything I can say to her. So, I will do all I can to prove that I would never harm her. That I will care for her and protect her with all that I am.

I listen as the sound of her breathing becomes soft and even, glad she trusts me enough to rest while I am nearby. It is a good sign, I believe, that she already understands I will not hurt her. And I vow I will never betray this trust she has gifted me.

If the storm is gone in the morning, we can return to my people and begin a search for hers. I only pray they are still alive and have not been found by our enemies or still in the hands of the A'kai.

Closing my eyes, I allow myself to drift off.

A loud cry startles me awake, and I jerk up to sitting.

"No!" Lara cries out.

My eyes adjust quickly to the darkness, and I find Lara wrapped up in the blankets and thrashing on the bed.

She must be having a bad dream. Carefully, I place a hand on her forearm. "Lara?"

Her eyes snap open, wide with fear.

"It's me, Markus."

"Markus?" She blinks several times.

"You were having a nightmare."

"Why is it dark in here?"

I tap the control panel and dim light floods the room. She pulls the blankets and furs even tighter around her like a barrier. "I hate the dark," she whispers. "It reminds me of the cages."

Inwardly, I curse myself. I should have realized. "Forgive me," I whisper. "I will make sure the light stays on. I will program it into the settings on the panel."

I move to tap in the commands, but her hand on my forearm stops me abruptly. "Thank you, Markus."

"You are most welcome."

Despite the lights now being on, I do not miss the trembling of her body beneath the covers.

As a warrior, I have seen many terrible things. I am no stranger to nightmares myself. The acrid scent of her fear still lingers, and I wish only to offer her comfort. "Would like something to eat? Something to drink?"

She shakes her head.

"You said you are a navigator."

"That's right."

I tap the control panel and an image of the stars appear on the ceiling as they can be viewed from this world.

Her brow furrows. "How did you do this? Is that somehow able to see through the cloud cover?"

"No. This is one of the images I took after we first crashed here, when I was trying to determine where we were."

She peers up at the stars, her stunning gray-blue eyes wide with wonder.

I press another button and, now the image is suspended around us, as if we were standing amidst the very stars themselves.

She sits up, her mouth drifting open in fascination. She reaches her hand out, feigning touching one of the stars, and a beautiful smile lights her face as it begins to glow brighter. "This is incredible."

CHAPTER 8

LARA

Markus gestures to one of the stars. "Here is the star we've learned to use for navigation. If you align it with these two"—he points to them —"then you know your bearings are true."

I study them intently, committing them to memory. "What about this one?" I ask, pointing to a particularly bright one beside it.

"Ah." He smiles. "That is the star that gives me hope."

"Why?"

"It is one that can be viewed from Mosaura. It is part of the constellation of Kilena and Tormin."

"Who were they?"

"Kilena was the First Empress of our people, and Tormin was her bonded one. When they died, the Creator gave them a place in the heavens, from where they will always be able to look down upon and guide our people." He pauses. "Even now, I believe they watch over us. And knowing this... it is as though having a piece of our home close to our hearts, even here, reminding us the Creator still keeps us in the palm of his hand."

His words are beautiful, and my heart clenches at the sadness in his voice while he speaks of missing his home. As much as I miss Terra, it only feels like months that I've been gone. But for him, it's been years.

I turn to face him. "I'm sorry, Markus. I know how terrible it is to miss home."

He swallows hard and looks down at his hands. "Yes. My parents taught me all about the stars when I was a fledgling." A wistful smile crests his lips. "That is why I mapped these," he gestures to the stars floating above us. "It reminds me of them."

"My parents taught me all the constellations, too." Emotions lodge in my throat, but I, somehow, manage to speak around them. "My dad even made this rotating light so it seemed like the stars were floating on the ceiling of my room." I reach out and touch one of the stars, watching as it grows even brighter. "It was not anywhere near as realistic as this, but it was still lovely.

"When I moved into my apartment, my dad brought it to me. I used to fall asleep with it on sometimes." A tear escapes my lashes at the memory, but I quickly brush it away. "I can't stop thinking about my parents. I can't stand the thought that they probably think I'm dead. And part of me is afraid I may never see them again."

Markus turns to me. He places his hand atop mine and squeezes it gently. "We have not found a way off this planet, yet, but I do not doubt someday we will. And when that day comes, I vow I will do whatever I can to help you find your people and your world, Lara."

My heart clenches at his words. "Thank you, Markus." Tears sting my eyes, but I blink them back.

"Forgive me," he whispers. "I do not mean to upset you."

"You're not. I just—" my voice catches. "After everything I've been through, I never expected such kindness from another person. I—" Emotions tighten my throat and I cannot speak.

"It is difficult to come from a place of darkness and back into the light," he murmurs. His violet eyes meet mine. "I was captured by slavers."

I blink at him in astonishment. "You were?"

"I was forced to fight in the gladiator pits. I was not held for very long. But it was... enough time to realize that the horrors I witnessed and the things I endured should never be suffered by another. Ever. It is why I worked hard to become a Commander in the Mosauran Empire. Why I volunteered my ship to patrol the borders of our region of space. I wanted to free as many slaves as I could and end the lives of all the masters who had kept them."

Gently, I squeeze Markus's hand in mine. He understands my pain and he does not judge me for my tears. "Do the dark memories ever go away?" I ask, voicing aloud my greatest fear. My worry that I will never be able to move past them.

"It is hard to adjust to the light after having experienced such darkness. My nightmares have lessened, but I do not believe they will ever completely go away. I turned my pain into a weapon—something that can be used to fight against the evil that plagues our universe. It shaped my life and inspired me to excel as a warrior.

"I often wonder if I would have had this same motivation without that terrible experience, but it is not an answer I will ever find. It is impossible to change the past. All I can do is strive to live a life that helps others. Slavery is abhorrent in every possible way, and if I can prevent others from suffering this fate, I will."

His gaze holds mine. "I know you are lost and far from home, but never for one moment believe you are alone. The

Creator of all things crossed your path with mine. I will do all that I can to help you. And when the storm clears, my people and I will search for yours."

For all that I'd heard of his people, whispered among the masters and some of the other slaves, I was not sure what to expect, but it certainly wasn't what I see before me now. Despite his fierce and intimidating appearance, Markus is the kindest and most caring man I've ever met.

As his violet gaze holds mine, warmth fills my chest. As if my soul has found some sort of resonating chord with his. I remember my grandmother saying she felt this with my grandfather when they first met, but I'd never truly believed her.

But as I stare across at Markus, I realize now that I'd been wrong.

After a while, my eyelids become heavy, and I struggle to stay awake as I listen to the smooth, deep sound of his voice. Unable to stay awake any longer, I close my eyes and drift off to sleep.

When I wake, the snow is still falling all around us, dark clouds hanging thick overhead. The entire forest is blanketed in snow, and the barest amount of light tells me it must be dawn.

I marvel at the trees with their dark gray bark and red needle-like leaves, reminding me of the pines on Terra, but so much larger. The light blue sky is not quite the same shade as Terra, but close enough. The sun is a bit more orange here than yellow, not vastly different from what I'm used to back home.

We're near the base of two towering mountains at the

edge of the forest. Covered in snow, their peaks disappear in the dark gray clouds of an overcast sky.

I turn onto my side and realize I'm still holding Markus's hand. His sharp, black claws are retracted so as not to accidentally scratch me. I peer over the side of the bed and find him lying on the floor, fast asleep.

I take a moment to study him. Dressed only in dark pants and boots, my eyes travel over the thick planes of muscle lining his abdomen and chest. His wings are spread out beneath him, and I marvel at the dark-silver, leathery sails. His mouth is partially open, and I study the two rows of sharp fangs.

This man is lethal and, yet, as I study our joined hands, I cannot help but think on how compassionate and gentle he is. He barely knows me, but he went out of his way to comfort me last night and to point out the stars above this world so I wouldn't feel so lost.

As if sensing my eyes upon him, his open, and the moment they find mine, he gives me a sleepy smile.

I give him one in return as he sits up. "Good morning, Markus."

He lifts his head to glance at the sky through the transparent walls of our shelter. Flakes of snow dance and twirl on the wind, but it seems the storm has already passed. "Yes, it is."

He turns his head off to the side and narrows his eyes. "It seems the worst of the storm is over for us, but it is still between here and the rest of my warriors." He taps on the control panel again and sighs heavily. "I still cannot send a signal. I will try again later."

He retrieves some more dried meat and water for our breakfast. He places them on a tray and sets it on the bed. As we eat, he holds out a tablet to me. "This is a portable control panel. It works just like the one here in the wall." He gestures to the one near the bed. "If you will press your hand to the screen, I will code it to recognize your commands."

I place my hand on the tablet and watch as a green light moves across the display. "Good," he says, smiling. "Now the door is coded to recognize you, as is the main computer."

I study the jumble of glyphs scrolling across the screen. "I… don't recognize any of these symbols."

"Forgive me." He frowns. "I'd forgotten about this."

"About what?"

"Your language. It is not programmed into the translator matrix."

"Then… how am I able to understand you? And the A'kai, for that matter?"

His brow furrows. "The translator enables you to speak and understand programmed languages, such as Mosauran and A'kai without realizing it." He pauses. "Right now, you are speaking the most commonly used Mosauran dialect, because it is the one I am speaking."

I still. I'd never realized this. Closing my eyes, I concentrate and speak in Terran Common. "Can you understand me?"

He cocks his head to the side. "I do not understand your words. Is that your native language?"

"Yes," I reply, allowing the translator to form the Mosauran word on my tongue. "I cannot believe I'd never realized this was happening."

"It is impressive technology." He tips his chin up with pride. "It was first developed by my people. But, it has a few faults. It will not translate your language for me. And because your language is not programmed into it, it will not translate written words for you in mine." He pauses. "This is why first contact with any new species is difficult. It often takes many cycles for teams of translators to ensure the new species' languages are properly converted into each and every language for which the embedded translators are programmed."

"You mentioned I was speaking the most common dialect of Mosauran. How many are there?"

He sits back in his chair. "There are three main dialects in use throughout the Empire." He cocks his head to the side. "What about your people? Do you have multiple dialects?"

"Yes, but everyone learns Terran Common. More than a century ago, Terra—our home world—experienced great earth shifts and drastic climate changes. They could have been more devastating, but all the Terran governments got together and formed one United Planetary Government with a common language so we could work together to stabilize our planetary ecosystem."

"What is the climate like on your world now?"

"Some areas of the planet are like this." I gesture to the snow-covered terrain outside. "But others are warm with dense vegetation. Forests with great trees and mountains." A wistful smile crests my lips. "Terra is beautiful.... There is so much to explore and see. I miss it."

"It sounds fascinating," he says. "Mosaura is covered in great mountains and thick forests of trees similar to these, but green instead of red. Our homes and structures are carved into the sides of the great rock walls. We have lavender skies and an orange sun. The temperature is cool, and the air is often thick with moisture." He raises his head toward the sky. "Here, it seems to snow every day, but on Mosaura, it is rain we see most often."

He turns his attention back to the tablet. "I will teach you to read these symbols, if you would like."

"I would appreciate that."

He flashes a handsome smile. "We will begin your lessons this evening, then. For now, I will go out to search for your friends. You will be safe here while I am gone."

He starts for the door, but I call out, "Wait!"

He turns back to me. "What is it?"

"I'd like to go with you."

He cocks his head to the side to regard me. "You are certain?"

"Yes. I want to help search for my friends."

He turns to a compartment beneath the door control panel and pulls out a blaster and a knife. He holds them out to me. "Have you had any training with weapons and self-defense?"

"Yes," I reply, thinking back on the many hours spent learning these things for the Terran space program. At the time, all of us thought it was strange they required us to know how to handle weapons and defend ourselves. After all, we were supposed to only be explorers and the ones who transported people and cargo back and forth from Terra to Mars. It was a branch of the Terran military, but we never considered ourselves soldiers. Now, I understand the program leaders must have anticipated potential first contact with a hostile species.

I study the weapons. They are different from what I was used to on Terra.

"Come," he says. "Let us practice a bit so you can get the feel of your weapons and I can assess your abilities."

I follow him outside, and he leads me to an area not far from our shelter that seems to have seen much practice. Several of the trees have scorch marks marring their trunks. He points toward the nearest one. "Aim for that tree."

I glance down at my blaster, unsure how to turn it on. Sensing this, he moves to my side, the heat of his body radiating to mine from his closeness as he reaches across and taps something on the top.

"This will deactivate the safety."

It's hard to concentrate with him standing so close. His

masculine scent—a mixture of cinnamon and spice—surrounds me, filling me with warmth.

"Now, aim," he says, pulling me back from my errant thoughts.

I force myself to focus as I take aim at the tree and fire, hitting my mark on the first try. I turn to find him practically beaming at me. "This is good," he says. "It seems you have had much training. Now, we will see how you do with a laser blade."

CHAPTER 9

MARKUS

After about an hour, her skin is practically glowing with exertion. She is as skilled with a blade as she is with a blaster. This is good. My Ashaya is capable of defending herself. She may be small, but she is fierce as any Mosauran warrior. "That is enough for today. We will train again tomorrow."

Lara nods.

"You must stand back while I shift."

"Shift?"

"Into my draken form."

Her brow furrows. "What is that?"

I stare deep into her eyes. Although I know she is brave and strong, I also understand the first time anyone sees my people change forms, it can be a jarring experience. Lara has been through much, and I do not wish to give her any reason to fear me.

"I do not want you to be afraid. I vow I will never harm you."

"I know you won't."

My chest swells with pride at her words. Trust is essential between mates. I will never break hers.

She continues. "If you'd wanted to hurt me, you could have done so, many times over, since we first met. I know you're not going to hurt me, Markus. Whatever you look like, I'm not going to judge you. All right?"

Despite her words, I still worry. I do not want to see fear reflected in her eyes as I take draken form. But I will not hide this part of myself from her, either. If I want her to know me, I must show her who and what I am.

With a slight clench of my jaw, I nod. "I need you to stand back."

CHAPTER 10

LARA

I watch in disbelief as Markus slides his pants down his legs. Without meaning to, my eyes travel down his physique, and my brow furrows when I notice a strange line down his scales where the typical male anatomy would be.

That's strange.... But, I suppose he is alien. Why should I just assume he'd be similar to my people?

He frowns. "My appearance displeases you."

Although he says this as a statement, I recognize it is also a question. In truth, he's perfect. His entire body is exquisitely sculpted. His masculine shoulders are broad, tapering down to a narrow waist with rippling plains of muscle along his abdomen and chest. Thick cords of muscle wrap around his arms and legs. Aside from his missing anatomy, he's the very essence of male perfection.

"No," I barely manage as my cheeks flush with warmth. "You're just... different from my people."

His eyes sparkle with barely restrained amusement. "Well, you *are* an alien species."

I laugh. "*I'm* the alien?"

He nods before his expression sobers. "What is it about my appearance that troubles you?"

"I—" I open my mouth to respond but stop, not sure I really want to tell him. Without thinking, my eyes drop to the line on his body.

"Ah," he says. "My mating pouch."

"Mating… pouch?"

He dips his chin. "We are not like the V'loryns. Our *stav* does not extend from our bodies until we are ready to mate."

Aware my lips part in surprise, I quickly snap them shut. "Oh," is all I reply, not sure what else to say. Part of me can't believe that I'm even attracted to him. He's a Mosauran, and I'm Terran. We're completely different species. I doubt he'd be interested in me anyway.

He takes a few steps back, and I gasp, astounded, as he transforms in a whirl of dust and wind into a dragon, one taken straight out of a painting from ancient Terran lore.

An enormous dragon towers over me, covered in silver scales shimmering iridescent beneath the sun. He flicks his long, tapered tail and lowers his massive, horned head. A large, violet, reflective iris contracts and expands as it meets my stunned gaze.

His nostrils flare, drawing my scent in before he releases a quick huff of air, nearly knocking me back. A nervous laugh escapes me. "Markus?"

Tipping his head toward me, his lips quirking up slightly at the edges, exposing a hint of his long, dangerous fangs, and I laugh. "Are you smiling at me?"

He nods, and pulls his lips back even more, revealing two solid rows of fangs. It would be terrifying, if I didn't know it were him. I run my hand along his massive jaw. His scales are smooth like silk beneath my fingers, instead of rough like I'd imagined they might be. "You look just like a dragon from ancient Terran myth," I say absently.

"Draken."

The word sounds in my mind and I jerk my hand away. Dark memories resurface of every time an A'kai invaded my thoughts.

"What was that?" I ask, unable to hide the slight tremor in my voice. "Did you just speak in my thoughts?"

His brows rise in a look that tells me he is as surprised as I am he's speaking directly to my mind.

"Forgive me." He moves toward me, but I take a step back.

I fist my hands at my side to still their trembling.

He gives me a pained look. *"I vow I will never harm you. Please, forgive me."*

I study him intently, willing myself to relax. This is Markus. He's done nothing but protect and take care of me ever since we met. I reach out and rest my hand lightly again on his jaw. "I know you would never hurt me. I'm fine. I promise."

"I should have realized this could happen between us, Lara."

I don't understand. "Why? Do all your people communicate with each other like this?"

He shakes his head. *"Only Ashaya are able to speak in each other's minds."*

"Ashaya? What is that?"

"It means—" He stills, and his head whips toward the forest. *"Someone is coming. Get behind me."* He spreads his wings wide to shield me.

I try to look past him, but he's so massive I cannot see anything.

A high-pitched howl sounds throughout the forest, followed by a chorus of several more. If I didn't know any better, I'd think they were wolves.

"Lycaons."

"What are—"

"They are a race of shifters, similar to mine, but they take a different form."

Fear invades me as I think back on the werewolf myths. "Do they look like... wolves?" I ask, hesitantly. Part of me doesn't want to know, but the other part knows I must ask.

"What are wolves?"

"They—" I open my mouth to speak but stop abruptly as something moves off to the side.

I glance toward it and inhale sharply as two sets of glowing predatory eyes—two yellow, two orange— meet mine. With thick, gray and brown coats of fur, these things look like wolves but much larger than any I've ever seen on Terra.

Markus releases a bellowing roar, and they crouch low. A deep growl rumbles in the closest one's throat as his orange eyes remain locked on mine.

Crushing terror turns my blood to ice as I hold up my blaster, ready to shoot if they come any closer. "Stay back!"

The wolf cocks his head to the side to regard me, but he stays where he is.

Markus opens his mouth and releases a wall of fire in a circle all around us, causing them to jump back, followed by another thunderous roar that stops my heart.

The Lycaons turn and race away.

I watch them retreating in the distance and see one of them stop and turn back. His stare is pointed and holds mine a moment before he runs away.

My heart is pounding in my chest as Markus turns to me. He curls his tail around my feet and curves his massive wing over my body, sheltering me.

"You are safe. I will not let anything harm you."

I press myself into his side, nestling in the safety of his

warmth, relishing his strong masculine scent. "Are they dangerous?"

"The Lycaons are very protective of females. Even ones outside of their species. And they abhor slavery, just as my people do. But I worry they may try to take you."

"Why?"

A low rumble emanates from his chest. *"Your hands are like ice. Why did you not tell me you were so cold?"*

"I—"

Without warning, he creates distance between us and shifts forms again. With one arm wrapped around me, he lifts his other hand to cup my jaw, tipping my face up to his. "We must make sure you are warm before we leave."

He takes my hand, leading me back inside our shelter. My jaw goes slack as I dart an appreciative glance at his very muscular backside. I snap it shut as my gaze moves over the rest of him. From his height, broad shoulders, and the lethal grace of his muscular form, I would know he's a warrior even if I'd never heard anything about his people before.

When we enter the shelter, he pulls two of the largest furs off the bed and wraps them around me like a cloak.

The leather hangs down to my ankles, and he rips another strip of my slave dress and ties it around my waist. "There"—cinching it just a bit more—"that should keep you warm."

While the fur is warm, it's bulky, making me puff out to almost twice my size. When we step outside, though, the cold is no longer biting, so I'm definitely not going to complain.

Markus turns to me again and cinches my make-shift belt even tighter. Just the extra gesture of concern makes my heart flutter in my chest. And when his violet eyes meet mine and he smiles, I can't help but smile in return.

"Better?"

"Much. Thank you."

My expression falls, however, when I glance down at the large wolf tracks in the snow.

"The Lycaons—your people don't get along with them?"

"Prior to crashing on this world, we rarely encountered them. They are a mostly nomadic race of mercenaries. We have avoided one another since the last Great War."

"Why did you think they might try to take me?"

"Because their Alpha—Luken—was emitting a pheromone. Did you not smell it?"

"No."

He cocks his head to the side to regard me. "Curious," he mumbles more to himself than to me. "It is usually a potent and irresistible lure for many females—even ones that are not Lycaon."

Those wolves were terrifying. I don't like the idea of being lured and then trapped because of a pheromone. I just escaped one captor, I don't want any others. "I won't be taken again," I whisper, more to myself than to Markus.

"Do not worry," he says confidently. "They are no match for a Mosauran." He surveils the sky. "Come. We will make a sweep of the surrounding forest."

Markus walks a space away, and I watch in stunned silence as he transforms again into a massive dragon. *Draken* —I correct myself. He kneels down and extends his leg for me to climb up onto his back.

I settle between his shoulders, looking for a way to hold myself steady during flight. I grab onto a few of the hard spikes protruding from the back of his neck, gasping when I realize how sharp and rigid they are. Sensing my concern, he slaps them flat against his back.

"Better?"

"Yes."

I marvel again at how his scales are soft as silk and how

beautifully they shimmer when the clouds part just enough to allow sunlight to hit them.

"You're so beautiful," I whisper more to myself than to him.

He turns to me, arching a very large brow. *"Not exactly the words a male wants to hear from a female."*

I laugh. "Ruggedly handsome then?"

His lips pull back in a dragon smile and he tilts up his chin, puffing his chest out with pride. *"You forgot to mention brave and strong."*

I laugh even more.

His entire body shudders beneath me, and a puff of smoke curls out around his nostrils as he laughs.

"Are you ready?"

I grab hold of one of his flattened spikes to secure myself. "Yes, I am, my ruggedly handsome, brave, and strong Mosauran," I tease.

He tips his chin up even higher as if preening at my words. I suppose it's a universal thing: all men love to be praised for their appearance and bravery. In Markus's case, it's well earned.

Powerful muscles flex beneath me when he extends his wings. A whirl of snow dances around us as his wings billow out like great sails, lifting us off the ground.

Cool air whips around me, in sharp contrast to the comforting warmth of his body, as we climb above the trees. He dips to the left and slips into a current, spiraling up toward the clouds.

I observe the beautiful landscape beneath us, the rays of the sun spreading across the snow in brilliant shades of red and orange. "This is amazing, Markus."

I've always loved flying, but this is something entirely different. It is complete and utter freedom unlike anything I've ever known.

Spreading his wings, he glides effortlessly above the forest. Strong wind claws at me, trying to rip me from his back, but I flatten myself against him and hold tight. I gaze down at the ground below. It would be a terribly long drop if—

"Do not worry," his mind whispers to mine, having sensed my fears. *"I would never let you fall."*

A smile crests my lips because I do not doubt his word.

Movement catches my eye in the distance, and I tap his neck to get his attention. "Off to the left," I tell him. "There's something there."

He turns toward it and tucks his wings to his body, my stomach dropping as he dives to investigate.

A creature comes into focus. With thick, snow-white fur, it's so large it reminds me of a snow leopard but solid white.

"A snowcat."

Glancing down at my coverings, it suddenly dawns on me why the fur looks so familiar.

He dips down behind it and draws in a deep breath. Before I can ask what he's doing, he releases a stream of flame, burning it instantly.

My jaw drops as we continue on, leaving the fiery carcass behind. "What was that for?" I ask.

He turns back, a curious look in his eyes. *"We must let it cook for a while before we retrieve it."*

"The smoked meat." The words escape my lips before I even realize I've said them aloud.

"Yes," he answers. *"You liked it, so I found you some more."*

I swallow thickly. It's one thing to eat an animal but entirely another to watch it be killed. Drawing in a deep breath, I force myself to push aside my disgust. If I'm going to survive here, I have to accept that food is not something easily come by on a planet this harsh.

One of the first things we learned during training for the

Terran space program is we have to adapt and overcome. As I survey the planet beneath us, determination steels me. I will do whatever it takes to forge a new life in this world.

We continue over the forest but find nothing else. I notice a lake of glistening, blue water below with steam rising from the surface. "What's that?" I ask, pointing toward it.

"A warm spring. We can bathe there if you'd like."

The ion shower in the pod was quick and efficient, but water sounds even better. "Is it safe?"

"I will protect you, Lara."

Not exactly the answer I was hoping for, but after what I saw earlier with the Lycaons, I don't doubt he can protect me.

He dips his wing, spiraling down toward the water. He touches down on the shore so gently I barely feel the landing. He kneels, and I start to slide off his back, but he shifts from draken form and wraps his hands around my waist, lowering me the rest of the way.

Even here on the shoreline, I can feel the heat radiating from the springs, and it feels so good I can hardly wait to get in. It's been ages since I had a real bath.

I look to Markus. "Will you turn around until after I get in?"

He gives me a curious look a moment before he nods and turns his back to me.

CHAPTER 11

MARKUS

I listen to the slight rustle of the fabric and furs as they drop to the ground. My stav presses insistently to the inside of my mating pouch as I imagine running my hands over her form, worshipping her as we—

With a slight clench of my jaw, I push this thought away. She is my Ashaya, but that does not mean she has agreed to become my mate. I must speak with her about this, but now is not the time. She has been through much, and I will not add to her burdens with my longing and desire.

I want only to protect her and keep her safe. Turning back toward the direction of my territory, I clench my jaw at the dark clouds covering the sky. The storm still lingers directly in the path we must take to reach my warriors, and I am desperate for it to clear.

Only when we return to my people will I know for certain she is well-protected against all threats.

A small splash tells me she has entered the water. A soft

sigh of contentment escapes her lips, and my entire body flushes with warmth at the enticing sound.

The dense forest surrounds us on all sides, and I continually scan the area for any sign we are being watched. When I am satisfied we are alone, I turn and walk into the water as well.

Lara's eyes watch me as I settle beneath the surface. I slip underneath to rinse my hair and face.

Lara obviously trusts me, but I know she is shy about her body. In this way, her people are much like the V'loryns. So, I do my best to keep my back to her, pretending I am not hyperaware of every ripple in the water with each movement she makes.

The wind picks up and my nostrils flare, detecting a familiar scent on the breeze. My eyes narrow and a muffled growl rumbles my chest. Moving in front of Lara, I spread my wings wide to shield her. "Show yourself, V'loryn."

Lara inhales sharply, but I cannot turn back to her now.

A male steps from the shadows of a nearby tree, his glowing, green eyes staring at me intently. "What are you doing with one of my people?"

With his pointed ears, short-cropped black hair, and slight scruff of beard, I recognize Commander Vorek immediately.

We were once as close as brothers. The bonds between us forged through shared suffering when we were both enslaved and forced to fight in the gladiator pits.

He was captured while searching for his sister after she was taken by slavers.

V'loryns are known far and wide for their stoicism. Their faces are perfect, impassive masks. It is believed they are a race incapable of emotion.

The day Vorek learned of the death of his sister is the day I learned this belief about his people was far from the truth.

But as I study him, it feels as if that was so very long ago. I wonder if he even still considers me his friend. Surely not. Too much has happened between us over these past several cycles. I know he still blames me for us having crashed on this world. I would take it back if I could, but the past is unchangeable.

"She is not V'loryn," I state firmly.

He cranes his neck and furrows his brow, straining to see behind me. "Are you all right?"

"Yes, I'm fine" Lara replies.

His eyes squint in doubt, and I bristle. "She is *not* my prisoner, Vorek."

"I did not accuse you of holding her against her will," he replies. "I merely wanted to offer her sanctuary with her people. *My* people," he emphasizes. "We have a settlement not far from here," he tells her. "If you come with me, we—"

"No," I grind out. "She will not go with you. She is safer with me."

His eyes swirl from glowing green to pitch-black, obsidian orbs. His fangs lengthen, and his nails extend into sharpened claws as he glowers at me.

From his aggressive appearance, if not for his pale skin and dark hair, I would almost think him A'kai. It is rare for a V'loryn to show any emotion, much less anger.

A sharp gasp draws my attention to Lara, standing behind me, her eyes glued to Vorek. "A'kai," she says, her voice barely a whisper as all the color drains from her face.

The acrid scent of her fear floods my nostrils, and my heart clenches when I notice her trembling. I wrap a protective arm around her. "No. He is V'loryn. He will not harm you."

Vorek's mouth drifts agape as his eyes return to their normal glowing green. He retracts his fangs and claws. "Forgive me. I did not wish to scare you. I—"

"She is mine, Vorek. Now, go."

He blinks several times, and it is easy to read the confusion etched across his normally impassive face. "Yours? Since when do Mosaurans take mates outside of their race?"

I clench my jaw. "Leave. Now."

"I *will* not," he protests. "If she is not one of my people, what species is she?"

"She is Terran. She and several of her kin were on an A'kai slave ship when it got caught in the wormhole, just as we were all those cycles ago."

His eyes widen. Everyone knows the horrors slaves endure at the hands of their A'kai masters. Sadness flits briefly across his expression, before he quickly retrains it into the impassive mask that is typical of his people, and I know he is thinking of his sister.

"The pods that fell from the sky," he murmurs. He tilts his head to the side. "How many have you found?"

"Only her."

He steps forward and regards Lara. "You are welcome to come with me if you wish. Our people will keep you safe."

Fierce possessiveness fills me, and I growl low in my throat.

Her hand on my arm makes me still. "No. I'm staying with Markus."

Vorek's gaze travels over me, his eyes narrowing as they meet mine.

Something dark and primal rises within me at her words. She trusts me more than a male who appears closer to her own species, and my heart swells with pride at this knowledge.

"Will you inform the Aerilons, when you return to your territory, about Lara's people?" I ask, satisfaction moving through me as I recognize the shock that flickers across his face. He did not realize my people know he is working with the Aerilons.

He levels an icy glare at me. "Have you been spying on us again?"

I straighten and puff out my chest. "It is important to know what your enemy is doing at all times."

"Is that what we are, Markus? Enemies?"

His words give me pause. I open my mouth to speak, but he interrupts.

"We are *not* at war. Our people had a treaty of nonaggression between us, last I understood. And you and I were—" he stops abruptly and then clenches his jaw. "Let us not forget *you* are the reason we are trapped here, Markus."

"Leave," I growl. "While you still can."

He draws in a deep breath. "Fine." He glances at Lara. "I will inform my people and the Aerilons about yours. If we find any, rest assured we will protect them."

"Thank you."

His piercing gaze holds mine a moment before he turns and races back through the woods.

I turn back to Lara and notice how pale she appears. "Are you all right?"

"Yes."

The scent of her fear is thick in the air, but she hides it well as she tips her chin up and looks to me. "Let's get back to the shelter."

When we reach the pod, the moment we get inside, Lara turns to me. "Why do Vorek's people look so much like the A'kai?"

"They are believed to share a common ancestor." I pause. "But they have very different cultures, now."

"How so?"

"The V'loryns used to be like the A'kai—ruthless conquerors and blood drinkers. But, now, they follow a different path. Their people do not express emotion. They can be cold and calculating. They hide the truth behind their impassive expressions and stoic features."

"They are your enemies?"

"We have a treaty of non-aggression between us, but my people do not trust them. Nor do theirs trust mine."

"And the A'kai?"

"They are enemies to all," I state firmly. I gesture for her to sit. "There is much I must tell you."

She takes a seat, and I retrieve more smoked meat and water and hand her a platter. I sit across from her and pull up a display.

With a flick of my wrist, I project the image of an Aerilon male in the space between us. Bitter jealousy rises within me as she studies the image of him in wonder.

"This is an Aerilon," I tell her. "I believe it would be best if you are familiar with the different species that reside on this planet."

"They're so beautiful," she says, and I can only hope she is speaking of his crystalline wings spread out in display behind his back. I hope she is not speaking of his green skin or his muscular form and square jaw.

I glance down at my dull, silver scales. They are nothing special, and I know most Mosauran females prefer a male with vibrant colors and markings. I hope that is not the case with Lara.

I quickly shut off the display, not wanting her to stare at the male anymore.

She looks to me. "What do the Lycaons look like when they're not... in the form they were today?"

I pull up an image of a Lycaon in two-legged form. With golden skin, slightly pointed ears, fangs, and a muscular form and glowing yellow and orange eyes, they look a bit like the

V'loryns, but there is enough difference to tell them apart rather easily.

I show her the differences between the V'loryns and the A'kai, projecting an image of them side by side. I point to the screen. "They have similar features," I explain, gesturing to their sharply pointed ears, their claws and fangs, their glowing green eyes and the three slight cranial ridges on their forehead. "But the A'kai have green skin and either white or dark hair. The V'loryns have skin tones anywhere from pale to dark brown and their hair colors vary as well from blond to black."

She studies the image a moment and then turns to me. "You and Vorek seem to know each other well."

Her statement, I recognize is also a question. "Yes. We were once as close as brothers. We were enslaved together and forced to fight in the gladiator pits."

"What happened between you?"

"After we escaped..." I lower my head as the memories flood my mind. "When we returned to our people, I suppose... it was easy to forget the brotherly bonds we'd shared during our captivity.

"There is a long history of mistrust between our Empire and theirs." I clench my jaw. "When we each returned to our people, it became... difficult to remember what had been built between us and—"

"You grew apart," she says, finishing my sentence.

I nod and she takes my hand, squeezing it gently. "Maybe someday you can rebuild your friendship. Perhaps—"

I shake my head. "I have tried, but to no avail."

CHAPTER 12

LARA

It's easy to read the sadness in Markus' features as he speaks of Vorek. I want to know more about what happened between them, but I also don't want to push Markus to talk about something that is obviously painful for him.

As I scroll through the various images on the screen. It's so strange how all these different races look like beings we regard as myths on Terra: Dragons, Elves, Vampire, Fae, Werewolves.

"What is wrong, Lara?"

"Nothing," I reassure him. "It's just that your people and the others… they look so much like creatures my people believe are only myths and legends."

He frowns. "It is possible our races may have come to your world long ago. But, if that is truth, I do not understand why they would not have stayed and conquered it for their empires."

"Are all of these other races your enemies?"

"It is… not that simple."

"What do you mean?"

"We have been in various states of conflict with each other for thousands of cycles." He pauses. "We have a treaty of non-aggression with the V'loryns and the Aerilons, but… as I mentioned, there is still much mistrust between us."

I sigh. "There's so much about this part of the universe I don't know." A faint smile tips my lips. "As a navigator, I hate the idea of being lost."

He leans forward. "What would you like to know?"

"Everything."

He flashes a handsome grin. "Then, I will do my best to tell you."

Markus begins giving me the history of his people and the others. It is interesting how these five races have been at odds with one another for so long. Even now that they have a treaty of nonaggression, they still continue to mistrust each other.

He pulls up an image of a male Mosauran. With silver-gray scales like Markus and silver eyes, it's the long, jagged scar on his face that draws my attention. It starts just above his right brow, stretching down to his cheek. I wonder how he didn't lose an eye to this injury. "Who is this?"

"That is Prince Soran of Mosaura," he says solemnly. "I met him when I was enslaved. We were owned by the same master, for a while, and forced to fight in pairs in the gladiator pits."

My mouth drifts open. "Did you say 'prince'?"

"Yes."

"Is that how he got that scar on his face?"

He nods. "An A'kai paid our master to allow him to fight the prince. He wanted to prove himself against a warrior of Mosaura. When the prince won, the A'kai ordered his men to hold him down so he could scar his face with a silic-acid tipped blade, dishonoring him and ensuring that no female Mosauran would ever want him as her mate."

"Mosauran women are that vain?" I ask incredulously.

"Most of them are." He pauses. "It was a terrible thing to do to him. He is a good and honorable male. He did not deserve what happened. His betrothed rejected him because of this scar. He had longed for her all those cycles during his slavery, only to be rejected the moment she saw it on his face."

I turn my gaze to the image of the scarred prince. My heart breaks for him. I can't imagine how devastating that had to have been.

My thoughts drift to the jagged scars that line my back— my slave markings. I reach up and absently trace the one across my shoulder. "Do Mosauran men look down upon scars too?"

His eyes meet mine intently. "Even before I was given my slave markings, I never judged another for their scars. For I understand that everyone, who has been through battle, carries them. Some are visible on the flesh but others leave their mark upon the heart."

"How did the prince get captured?"

"Enemies of the crown killed his father and sold him into slavery. His mother—the Empress—believed him dead."

"Were you both rescued together?"

"No. Shortly after I escaped my slavery, I went to his brother, Prince Rowan, and told him about Soran. I explained that we had fought together in the arenas and that I believed him to still be alive.

"I helped him find Prince Soran. It was shortly after that when the Empress granted my request to have my ship assigned to patrol our borders and enforce our anti-slavery laws."

"Did the prince ever find a mate?" I ask, my heart still bleeding for this man that I don't even know.

"No, he did not." He sighs. "At least... not before we crashed on this planet. It has been ten cycles since we were both freed. Perhaps, he may have found someone by now, I hope. He is a good and honorable male. After all he endured, he deserves to be happy."

Sadness tightens my chest as I look to Markus. I wonder if he was rejected by someone for the scars on his back. "Did you have someone waiting for you when you were rescued?"

The moment the question leaves my mouth, I wish I could take it back. I shouldn't have asked him this. I don't want to dredge up any painful memories for him.

"No, I did not. Most females prefer a male with vibrant colors and markings." He looks down at himself. "My coloring is rather dull and unattractive among my people."

"What are you talking about? You're beautiful, Markus."

The green on his cheeks and brow darken at my words even as he arches a teasing brow. "I thought we agreed that I was ruggedly handsome."

"We did." I laugh. "Ruggedly handsome, brave *and* strong." I take his hand and meet his gaze evenly. "I mean it, you know. Any woman would think so."

A gorgeous smile lights his face. He puffs out his chest and tips his chin up with pride.

"Now you're just showing off," I tease him.

We both laugh before turning our attention back to the console.

He pulls up a map on the display and holds it up to me. "These are the various areas of the planet we have charted, so far. Here"—he points to a tiny dot on the screen—"is our shelter." He traces a line toward a towering mountain. "This is the mountain our ship crashed into. We have claimed it and created a network of tunnels to serve as our compound, here."

"What is this area?" I point to a location not far from this one.

He frowns. "That is the V'loryn's territory." He points to another area beside it. "And this belongs to the Lycaons."

I glance at the shelter then look to him. "It seems like you still have use of quite a bit of technology, despite being stranded here."

"We scavenge what we can, and our engineers have been able to repair many of our ship's functions."

"But, no one has been able to repair their ship so they can try to leave?"

Drawing in a deep breath, he turns his focus to me. "Each of us has tried. Our ships were badly damaged. None have the power necessary to break atmosphere. Our distress signal has gone unheard all these cycles." He sighs. "We are fortunate we are even able to have communications on this world. At first, the mountains made it difficult. There is an ore that lies beneath the ground that is similar to something found on our world that impairs communication equipment. We placed enough relays along the peaks to broadcast signals over longer distances, but it is not reliable. And the storms here can be violent and they are very unpredictable; unlike anything we have encountered on any other known worlds in our Empire. This does not help either."

He lifts his gaze to the sky. "As soon as the storm clears between here and my people, I will try again for a signal. Until then, I will show you how to navigate the computer."

I'm eager to learn all that I can. "Thank you. That would be wonderful."

I've always been fiercely independent. Learning how to use his people's technology makes me feel as if I have control again over my life and my future. For so long, I lived at the whim of others—my masters. But now, I am free. Free to choose the path that will guide me to my future.

As Markus teaches me the various symbols on the screen and explains their meanings, he flashes a devastatingly handsome smile when I choose the right one to pull up the communication relay.

Despite the fact that it is not working right now, due to no signal, my chest swells with pride.

His reflective violet gaze meets mine and, despite only knowing him for a few days, I realize just how easy it would be to get lost in his eyes.

Something about him draws me in. I never believed in love at first sight, even after my grandmother told me about how she fell for my grandfather. She claimed their souls were connected, right from the start.

I shouldn't be thinking about things like this. I should be focusing solely on learning how to survive here and finding my friends. But each time Markus smiles at me, I feel an answering tug in my heart. As if I've known him all my life even though we just met.

I don't understand it, but something deep in my soul recognizes him. As if we are tethered by some invisible cord between us. I don't know if he feels this way too, or if it's only in my head. But when he speaks my name and takes my hand in his, I wonder what it would be like to hold onto him forever.

CHAPTER 13

MARKUS

She is curious, not only about this world and about my culture but also the others. Her mind is sharp, and I am surprised by how quickly she is already recognizing the various symbols of our language as I teach her to navigate the computer.

She is very skilled with a blaster and a blade, for which I am grateful. I have no doubt she is able to defend herself. Despite all she has been through, she presses on, determined to learn how to survive on this world. This speaks to her strength of will that rivals that of a Mosauran warrior.

She presses the correct symbol on the screen to access the terrain charts and turns to me with a beaming smile that could rival the brightness of the sun. Her radiant gray-blue eyes stare into mine, and I am lost in their depths.

As the night wears on, her eyelids blink open and closed more slowly. When she falls asleep in the chair, I carefully lift her into my arms and place her in the bed. I tuck the furs over her shoulders, taking a moment to study her.

Her long, brown hair is spread out beneath her on the pillow like a beautiful halo. Long lashes fan over soft, pink cheeks and her mouth is slightly open in a small O.

She is intelligent, beautiful, strong and brave. Even if she were not my Ashaya, I would still desire her as mine. Lara is everything I could ever wish for in a mate.

But she is not my mate and might never wish to be. As I gaze at her, renewed determination fills me. I have already lost my heart to her. Maybe it is the bond that makes me feel this way so soon. Even if it is, it does not matter. It does not change the truth I understand deep in my soul. Lara is mine and I am hers. Now, I must do whatever I can to prove to her that I am worthy to be her mate.

Long ago, my ancestors used to hoard treasure in their dwellings, many of them amassing great wealth and defending it with their lives.

Inhaling deeply, I draw her delicate scent deep into my lungs. Gently, I brush a stray tendril of hair back from her face. She is more precious than any treasure, and I would give anything to be hers.

CHAPTER 14

LARA

It has been five days. The storm is still raging between us and Markus's people. It's strange a storm would last this long, but I realize I am on an alien world. Markus assures me it is common and will probably lift soon, but I'm a bit nervous about when it finally will.

I'm comfortable with Markus. I'm just not sure I want to be around others just yet. I like that it's just us. I don't know how it will be when we return to his people. He's their Commander, and I'm sure he'll be busy much of the day.

He probably won't have as much time to spend with me, but it's more than that. Even though we haven't known each other very long, I love spending time alone with him. We talk about everything and nothing, and every time he smiles at me lately, my heart skips a beat.

He's handsome and kind and intelligent and caring—everything I would have looked for in a Terran man, had I gotten around to really dating. I'm falling for him, against my better judgment.

I'm worried I'll end up with a broken heart. We're two different species. I doubt he is interested in me in that way.

After breakfast, I follow him outside. He turns to me. "You are skilled with weapons. Now, we will see how you do in hand-to-hand combat. Are you ready?"

"I'm ready."

He moves into a defensive stance, and I do the same as we circle one another. "Defend yourself," he says and rushes toward me.

I spin away at the last moment. He wastes no time attacking again, and I duck beneath his grasp. I sweep out with my foot and hook the back of his ankle, causing him to stumble forward.

When he recovers and turns to face me, I note the smile that quirks his mouth. "You are good. You use your smaller size to your advantage, forcing me to adjust my movements in such a way it challenges my balance." His expression becomes focused, staring at me intently. "But do you know how to break free of a hold?"

I still. Dark memories fill my mind of the time I tried to escape the A'kai. One of them held me, locked in a hold that I could not break out of, no matter how hard I tried.

He could have easily taken control of my mind to stop me, but he enjoyed feeling me struggle against him. He took sick delight in my panic and fear as I tried and failed to free myself.

"Know I will never harm you, Lara," Markus says, pulling me back from my dark thoughts. "What I do is meant only to teach you to protect and defend yourself. Do you understand?"

I nod affirmatively.

"Are you ready?"

I swallow hard. It's on the tip of my tongue to say 'no,' but he's right. I have to learn this. I *want* to learn this.

"Yes," I lie.

In a blur of movement, he rushes forward. He spins around to my back so quickly I don't even realize what's happened until he has me completely immobilized. With my back to his front, he has one arm banded around my waist, pinning my arms to my sides, the other across my chest so his other hand grips my chin firmly, locking me in place.

Horrible memories pierce my thoughts, and I struggle against his hold. Fear wells up within me, panic taking hold. Tears sting my eyes and blur my vision as I try, but fail, to hold back a whimper. "Let me go," I barely manage.

He releases his grip immediately and moves in front of me. His violet eyes search mine, pain evident behind them. "Forgive me, Lara. I—"

"It's not you. It's just—" my voice catches, and I'm unable to speak past the dark memories filling my mind.

CHAPTER 15

MARKUS

She does not finish her sentence, but she does not have to. I can only imagine what she must have experienced during her time as a slave.

I take her hand gently in mine. My heart clenches as she bravely blinks back the tears that would fall, were she to let them. "It is all right. It will take time to heal, Lara. Given all you went through, it is to be expected you would—"

"Be weak?" her voice quavers. "I don't want to be weak. Not anymore. I can't afford to."

The pain in her expression nearly breaks me for I recognize it well. I cup her chin, tipping her face up to mine. "Many warriors have scars from battle. Not just physical ones, but ones that are carried in here." I place my hand over my heart. "When my people fight, we make a pledge to each other. In battle your team is only as strong as the weakest among you. We vow to one another that if one of us falls injured, we will carry them to victory or to death. We will not leave them behind."

I continue. "I understand what it is to carry dark and terrible memories. The things you have suffered will never fully leave you. Those types of scars remain. They become part of you... shaping who you are as you learn how to carry them."

Tears fills her eyes, but she blinks them back.

Her gaze holds mine as I take her hand. Threading my fingers through hers, I stare deep into her eyes. "I will carry you, Lara Martin, to victory or to death. I will not leave you behind. We are bound to one another, and if you are broken, so am I."

A tear slips down her cheek as I continue. "I know you are lost, but you have also been found. You are not alone. I am here, and I will remain at your side for as long as you will have me. I promise to do everything I can to help you to heal and to find your way in this life. I give you my most solemn vow as a warrior of Mosaura."

She cups my cheek. Her blue eyes search mine a moment before she leans in and presses her soft lips to my own.

I still, unsure what to do.

"I'm sorry. I shouldn't have done that."

I cup her cheek and run the soft pad of my thumb across her full lower lip, staring at her in wonder. "What was that? This touching of lips?"

"A kiss," she whispers. "Do your people not kiss?"

I shake my head. "What does it mean?"

"It doesn't matter. I... shouldn't have done it."

"Lara, please tell me what it—"

"I'm sorry, Markus. Forget it happened." She clears her throat and takes a small step back.

My entire body warms at the memory of her mouth upon mine. How am I supposed to forget such a thing happened? It was unlike anything I've ever experienced before.

Although I want to ask more about her kiss, I do not press her further. I will respect her wish to not speak of it.

Her gaze drops to my mouth once more. *Love*—the word flashes through my mind and I realize it has come from her, through our bond.

Could it be that she loves me as I love her?

She gifted me the intimate touch of her lips to mine. Although she would not explain, I suspect such a thing carries great importance to her. I have seen the Aerilon do this, but only between mates.

My heart soars and I am barely able to focus as we continue with our lessons. My mind keeps returning to the feel of her mouth and the warmth of her breath on my skin.

Lara is everything I could ever want in a mate. Now, I must do all that I can to convince her to be mine. I will buff my scales when I use the ion cleanser next. Females appreciate a male who takes great effort with his appearance. I hope it will impress her.

CHAPTER 16

LARA

By the time we are finished, snow begins to fall heavily all around us. Dark clouds are spread out like a thick blanket overhead. "We should go back into the shelter until this passes," Markus says.

Reluctantly, I agree. I'd rather continue my training, but the weather is getting worse.

After our kiss, I'm not sure I want to be confined to such close quarters with him. I don't trust myself not to kiss him again.

Inwardly, I wince. He didn't know what it meant and I... shouldn't have done it. I risk ruining the friendship I have with him. If he doesn't want me like I want him, things will get awkward between us, and that's the last thing I want.

I go into the cleansing stall and press the button for the ion cleanser. It doesn't feel as good as a shower, or as bathing in the warm springs, but it's better than nothing. And, at least, I feel clean instead of sweaty, like I did earlier.

It doesn't do anything to clear my head, however. My mind keeps replaying our kiss.

After Markus uses the ion cleanser, we sit down across from each other. I notice his scales are buffed to a fine sheen. Brighter than I've ever seen them before.

I frown. "Your scales…"

"Yes?" His brows go up slightly.

"They're… very shiny."

A devastatingly handsome smile lights his face. "Thank you, Lara."

I assume what I said is a compliment, so I add. "They look nice."

He puffs his chest out with pride, and I force myself to suppress a laugh as he tips his chin up as well.

He's handsome and he knows it.

I bite back a sigh. I really need to get ahold of myself. He's just being friendly. Surely, he's not interested in me.

Clearing my throat, I think of something to talk about.

Something has been bothering me ever since we ran into Vorek—the V'loryn Commander. He mentioned their being stranded here was Markus's fault. I hadn't asked him about it then, but I want to know what happened.

I lean forward. "What did Vorek mean when he said it was your fault everyone is trapped here?"

With a slight clench of his jaw, he lowers his head. "My crew and I came across a stranded Aerilon ship just inside the edge of our region of space. The V'loryns were rendering aid, but we"—he stops abruptly—"I told them to leave immediately. They did not respond."

"So, what happened?"

"I recognized Vorek's ship. I thought he ignored me intentionally, expecting our… previous friendship to grant him immunity from our laws. Technically, they were both in violation of Mosauran territory."

"Why didn't they answer you?"

He sighs heavily. "The communications were down. Something shorted the circuitry on both ships when the V'loryns were rendering aid. I did not know this until... after."

"You couldn't have known."

He shakes his head. "Over the course of our history, there have been many conflicts between us in defense of borders and territories. My brother died during a skirmish with an Aerilon vessel. It clouded my judgment."

I take his hand in mine, observing the terrible pain etched in his features.

"I did not trust the Aerilons before then, and I certainly did not trust them after. I have a duty to protect those under my command. I worried it was some sort of trap."

"You fired on them."

"It was only a series of warning shots. I could not bring myself to command a direct hit." He clenches his jaw. "An A'kai ship decloaked out of nowhere and thought to take advantage of our situation. Then, the Lycaons came and joined the fight as well."

"Then, what happened?" I ask, curious to understand how they all ended up stranded here.

"The wormhole that brought us here—the same one that destroyed the ship you were on... it jumps locations. The end close to this planet is fixed to a subspace bearing, but the one at the other end is not. It is unstable and prone to drift. We had little warning when it moved to our location at the exact moment of fighting and pulled us in." He pauses. "I have tried to convince myself that it is the will of the Creator that we all ended up here... but, I cannot."

"You couldn't have known what would happen."

He lifts his violet eyes to me, his expression full of guilt. "I was the one who first fired upon their ships and began the conflict. I am the Commander, and it was my job to keep a clear head, and instead, I allowed my emotions to overrule rational actions." He runs a hand roughly through his hair. "My warriors have never blamed me. They are loyal to a fault. They work tirelessly, day and night, to carve out a life here while still searching for any way to repair our ship or to, at least, get a signal to home."

"I'm sorry, Markus. That's a terrible burden to carry."

He shakes his head. "An even worse one to know I do not carry it alone. My actions have shouldered this terrible consequence, not just on my warriors but upon the other races. Commander Vorek reminds me of this every time I see him… and, yet, I cannot blame him, because I know, were our roles reversed, I would do the same."

I cup his cheek. "Everyone makes mistakes, Markus."

"Not ones like this."

"I was the navigator of my ship. I was the one who charted the course that probably led to our being captured."

His brow furrows. "What do you mean?"

"Ours was not the first ship to disappear. There were many others before us over the past several decades, most of them lost along a certain flight path." I pause. "This particular path was the fastest route home. Most navigators avoided it because they believed it was bad luck."

He's silent as he waits for me to continue.

"I charted a path straight through it, because I wanted to get home in time to surprise my mom for her birthday." Tears swim at the edge of my vision, but I hold them back. "Because of me, we got taken while we were still in stasis. My entire crew were captured because of me."

"No, Lara. You cannot blame yourself for—"

"Don't you see? If you're responsible for what happened to your people, I'm just as liable for what happened to mine."

His violet gaze holds mine. He opens his mouth to speak

but stops abruptly, zeroing in on something outside the transparent walls. I turn to look but see nothing.

"What is it?"

"Stay here, Lara. I must go speak with them."

"Who are you talking about?"

The question barely leaves my mouth when I look outside and see two pairs of glowing eyes blinking back at me: one set yellow and the other orange. "Are those the—"

"Lycaons," he growls.

"Markus, don't go out there. Please."

"They already know we are here. They can scent us. They will not leave until I speak with them."

He reaches up to press his hand on the door panel, but I grip his forearm, stopping him abruptly.

"I'm going with you then."

He opens his mouth to protest, but I press a finger to his lips to silence him.

"The only way you're going out there is with someone to watch your back." I pat the blaster on my hip.

"Fine." He purses his lips. "But stay behind me."

"I will."

He turns back to the door, pressing his hand on the panel for it to slide open.

I watch the two Lycaons approach warily. Their lips are pulled back in a feral snarl, mirroring the same one on Markus's face, as they stalk toward us.

"Do not come any closer," Markus snaps.

They stop abruptly, and I watch in stunned silence as they shift into their two-legged form.

They appear similar to Terrans but much taller. But their golden skin, glowing eyes, pointed ears, and fangs remind me they're definitely not one of us.

The one with orange eyes steps forward. His entire body is layered with thick, corded muscle. As I glance down his form, I note he must have the same mating pouch the Mosaurans have, because I notice the same line in his skin, in the middle of his groin area.

He looks to Markus. "We came to warn you, Mosauran."

Markus growls, low and menacing.

He continues. "We have scented several A'kai near this area. We were hunting them to clear them from this place, but, so far, we have turned up nothing. We came to you in good faith so you might leave with your female. Take her back to your people where she will be safe."

Markus blinks at him, visibly stunned by his words.

The man runs a hand through his short, brown hair and shakes his head to remove some of the snow that has settled there. His glowing, orange eyes meet mine. "We thought you were V'loryn, but your scent suggests otherwise. What are you?"

Markus spreads his wings wide to shield me, but I place a hand on his back, and move to his side. "I am Terran."

He turns to his companion, and something unspoken passes between them.

He looks back at me. "I am Luken, and this is Dakor," gesturing to the one with yellow eyes.

"I'm Lara."

"We have also scented some of your people."

Frantic hope flares inside me. "Have you seen any others? Anyone like me?"

His expression turns grim, and my stomach falls with dread. "They are with the A'kai we are tracking."

"Do you know where they went?"

He shakes his head. "The A'kai are excellent hunters and know how to avoid becoming prey. They mask their scent and that of the females with them. We have caught a hint of it on the wind, but not enough to locate them. Yet."

Markus wraps a protective arm around me. "As one

warrior to another, I thank you for the warning. Now...
Leave."

Luken's eyes burn with indignation. "Do you not under-stand what I am telling you, Mosauran? We have scented more than one A'kai in these woods. Take the female and leave. Return to your people before it is too late or else, give her to us. Our pack will protect her, if you will not."

Markus releases a hostile rumble, pulling me behind him. "If you dare try to take my female, I will end you, Lycaon."

'My female.'

Markus's words surprise me, and yet, I'm not disturbed by his claim. If anything, it only makes me feel more protected and my heart skips a fluttering beat.

Luken bares his fangs in a feral snarl. "You are a fool, Markus."

Markus darts a glance over his shoulder, and Luken follows the line of his sight. "Do you not see the storm between us and my people?" He seethes. "I would take her to our territory now, if not for that. I refuse to risk her life braving a storm."

Luken blinks several times and gives him a reluctant bow of the head. "I did not realize."

A lone howl sounds in the distance, and Luken's ear turns toward it. He meets Markus's eyes evenly. "We are still hunting the A'kai. Do not stand in our way. You are not our target, Mosauran."

"Understood."

With that, Luken and Dakor shift back into wolf form and sprint away, disappearing into the darkness of the forest.

A shudder of fear moves through me, and Markus spins to face me, his violet eyes searching mine. "I can scent your fear. It is all right, Lara. They are gone."

I shake my head. "It's not them I'm afraid of."

He straightens. "The A'kai."

"Yes."

"We will remain in the shelter until it is safe to leave," he says. "The door is coded only to us. Even if the A'kai found us here, they cannot enter."

His words, I understand, are meant to reassure me, but I still can't help but be afraid. "Then, let's get back inside. I don't want to stay out here."

Markus guides me back into the shelter, sealing the door shut behind us.

"Lara, I—"

"They're monsters, Markus. The A'kai are monsters. We have to find my people before they—"

"We will," he says. "The Lycaons are already searching. I'm certain the V'loryns and Aerilons are, too. When we return to my people, we will have even more warriors who will join the search."

"Thank you," I whisper.

He cocks his head to the side. "For what?"

A smile tugs at my lips, despite my sadness. "For trying to make me feel better. For giving me hope."

He takes my hand in his. "There is always hope, Lara. We will not stop searching until we find your people. You have my most solemn vow as a warrior of Mosaura."

CHAPTER 17

LARA

The snow is still falling heavily outside. Markus gives me the bed again while he settles on the sofa. He's so thoughtful and caring. When he looks at me and smiles, bidding me goodnight, I realize just how easily it would be to lose myself in his violet eyes.

There's just something about him that draws me in. The more time we spend together, I find myself falling for him even deeper. But I doubt he feels the same, and I'm too nervous to ask him about it—afraid I'll ruin the friendship we have between us.

With a heavy sigh, I roll over onto my side and close my eyes. I need to get some sleep. Who knows what tomorrow may bring; I need to be ready for anything.

Falen's glowing, green eyes glare at me as he stalks forward, fangs bared. His eyes swirl into obsidian black with the extension of his claws. "You thought to escape me, you pitiful Terran," he snarls. "There is no escaping my kind."

He rushes forward and pins me to the ground. I choke on a scream as he buries his fangs deep into my neck.

"Lara! Lara!" Markus's voice startles me awake. He stares down at me in concern. "You were having a nightmare."

I jerk up to sitting and wrap my arms around him, holding him close. "I dreamed about Falen. The A'kai you—" my voice hitches.

Markus tightens his arms around me, his masculine scent of spice and cinnamon surrounds me. His breath is warm in my ear as he whispers. "You are safe, Lara. I will not let anyone harm you."

As he holds me, I nestle deep into his embrace. He holds me close and whispers soothingly in my ears, gently nuzzling my temple. "You should try to rest, Lara."

I lie back, and he tenderly covers me again with a heavy layer of furs to keep me warm. When he moves to stand, I grip his forearm, stopping him abruptly.

"Stay," I whisper, pulling back the covers.

His brow furrows in confusion, so I quickly amend. "Just to sleep. That's all."

He nods and crawls into the bed, beside me.

He lays on his back, his entire body tense, as if afraid to move.

I scoot closer to him and nestle against his body, resting my head on his shoulder and draping my arm across his chest, directly over his heart. Cautiously, he lays his hand atop mine, squeezing it gently.

Closing my eyes, I drift off to sleep, surrounded by the comfort of his body and his warm, cinnamon scent.

CHAPTER 18

MARKUS

I hold Lara close while she drifts off to sleep. She shivers slightly, and a crease forms between her brows, as though something in her dreams troubles her. I reach across and gently smooth it with my thumb, brushing the hair back from her face.

Carefully, I wrap my wings around her, holding her tight. She settles into me with a soft sigh that makes my heart clench. After all that she has been through, I am both surprised and honored by her trust that I will not harm her.

Drawing in a deep breath, I glance at the panel. It is several more hours before dawn. A lone Lycaon howl sounds in the forest, reminding me they still hunt the A'kai.

Despite the fact they are not friends of my people, I realize they are not enemies, either. It is comforting to know they hunt the woods for those monsters. It is, yet, another layer of protection for my Ashaya that they keep watch outside our shelter in this way.

I curl my wings a bit tighter around her as I listen to the soft sound of her breathing as she sleeps. Even if she never wants anything more, it would not matter to me. I am content to just hold her like this. And if she will let me, I will hold onto her forever.

CHAPTER 19

LARA

When I wake in the morning, I'm completely wrapped up in warmth. His wings are folded around us, my head on one arm and his other draped over my waist. With my back to his front, Markus is curled protectively around me.

I breathe deep of his masculine scent and marvel at the texture of his wings. I reach out and gently trace my fingers along the soft, leathery folds. "Beautiful," I whisper to myself.

"Not exactly what a male wants to hear from a female," his deep voice rumbles mockingly behind me, and I can hear the playful smile behind his words.

I turn in his arms and try, but fail, to restrain a teasing grin. "How about ruggedly handsome? We agreed on that earlier, remember?"

He dips his chin in a firm nod as a smile tugs at his lips. "We also agree on brave and strong as well."

"You're right." I laugh. "We did. My ruggedly handsome, brave and strong Mosauran warrior."

His expression turns serious as his gaze holds mine. "Yours," he agrees.

The silence stretches between us as his violet eyes search my own. My eyes drift down to his perfect, full lips, and I'm tempted to kiss him again.

As if sensing my thoughts, he leans in. The warmth of his breath fans across my face—a heady scent of cinnamon and spice. I'm already imagining the taste of his mouth as we drift closer.

At the last second, my nerves get the best of me and I turn away.

He pulls back too, and I wince inwardly.

Why didn't I kiss him? I wanted to but I… got nervous and now we're laying here together in awkward silence that is completely and utterly my doing.

Markus clears his throat and sits up on the edge of the bed.

I do the same as I gaze through the transparent ceiling of the protective pod. Flakes of snow twirl and dance on the breeze, but it is light enough we should be able to search for my people again today.

As if reading my mind, Markus turns to me. "We will eat, then we will fly over the forest, searching for any sign of your friends."

"All right."

CHAPTER 20

MARKUS

When we're finished eating, Lara begins to layer on her furs. I watch as she fights with her makeshift belt and wraps it around her waist. I insisted she wear extra layering and then watch as she waddles to the table and takes one last drink of water before returning to my side.

A smile tugs at my lips as I inspect her outfit. I gently smooth it out and cinch the belt a bit more to secure it. Terrans cannot regulate their body temperatures as efficiently as my people. I want to make sure she's completely covered and protected from the cold.

A smile lights her face. "Thanks, Markus."

As soon as we step outside, movement in the corner of my vision catches my eye. I snap my head in the direction of the motion but see nothing. Flaring my nostrils, I scent the air, searching for anything familiar.

I can smell nothing but the earth, the crisp, frigid air, and the trees.

"Is something wrong?" Lara's voice draws my attention back to her.

"No. I... thought I saw something for a moment, but I do not sense anything now."

Her eyes sweep out over the forest then turn to me. I note how she palms the blaster tucked into the belt around her waist. I am glad she carries this and her laser blade.

"You ready?"

I nod, and she takes a few steps back.

Closing my eyes, I allow myself to transform. My draken form is always ever-ready just beneath the surface, like a wild and untamed thing waiting to be freed. A thrill runs through me as I breathe deeply of the crisp, cold air and spread my wings. The deep stretch as they unfold from my body is a feeling unlike any other.

I look down at Lara, and she gives me a lovely smile. Kneeling to the ground, I extend my front leg for her to climb onto my back. As she settles over me, contentment thrums through my veins as my mind speaks to hers. *Are you ready?*

"Yes."

Extending my wings, I lift up and catch the wind in my sails. We climb above the tree line and head out over the forest. I dip my wing to the left and made a wide arc over the woods.

Lara leans to one side, extending her hand to skim the tops of the snow-covered trees. She makes a noise of pure joy as they explode in a rain of powdery, white dust, trailing behind us as we sail on the current.

I fly out over the frozen river and the icy plains on the other side. The sun paints the landscape with brilliant colors —oranges, yellows, and reds—beneath us. Something reflects in the distance, and I notice the moment Lara sees it, too, because she taps the back of my neck lightly to draw my attention. "Over to the right," she says. "There's something metal—some kind of reflection."

I dip my wing and sail toward it. As we draw closer, I realize it is an A'kai escape pod. I recognize the dark metal and the dart-like design.

She gasps, and I know she has realized this, too. Cautiously, I swoop low, checking for anyone nearby. Everything is still around it, and there is no evidence of any recent tracks around the vessel, indicating it is either abandoned or its occupants are still inside.

I land several lengths away, shifting into my two-legged form, wrapping my hands around Lara's waist, gently lowering her to the ground. I place my hands on her shoulders and meet her eyes. "Please, wait here while I investigate."

She frowns. "I don't want you to go alone."

I tip my head up and scent the air, nostrils flaring, but I cannot sense anything. With a slight clench of my jaw, I shake my head. "Please, stay."

She turns a worried gaze to the escape pod and looks back at me. She takes my hand, squeezing it gently. "Be careful, Markus."

I nod and start toward the vessel. As I draw closer, a hint of death and decay is carried on the breeze. Something is inside, but I cannot tell if it is one of her kind or the A'kai. Perhaps, it is both.

I wrinkle my nose as the stench grows stronger the closer I get. Cautiously, I approach, worried it could be some sort of trap.

I cast a quick glance over my shoulder to Lara and find her standing in the distance, blaster in hand, as though readying to defend us both.

The dark-metal hull glints beneath the sun like an ominous beacon in an ocean of ice and snow. We have flown over this area before, but it must have been covered. Deep claw marks on the viewscreen and hatch door tell me some sort of predator was here not long ago, trying to gain entry but to no avail.

I scan the ice and snow, searching for signs it still lingers nearby. There are many dangerous creatures on this planet, but most of them avoid me and my kind, recognizing we are the superior predators here now.

I climb up the side of the pod and scrape away the fine layer of snow covering the hatch glass. I peer inside, and my eyes widen as I notice the slumped-over body of an A'kai strapped to one of the seats.

I grip the hatch door handle firmly and wrench it open. My eyes swim as putrid air escapes and fills my nostrils. I notice no one else inside. As I spin the chair, I note the blaster scorch mark across his chest and the burned flesh all around it. This A'kai was shot point-blank by someone.

A smile tips my lips as I detect the subtle scent of a Terran. I recognize this, now I've been around Lara long enough to distinguish it from that of the other races. This monster must have been killed by his captive, and I am glad.

I scan the stark landscape around us. I wonder where she is—this brave Terran who shot her master.

I climb down and half jog, half glide with my wings over to Lara's side. Her eyes are wide as she looks to me. "What did you find?"

"A dead A'kai. It looks like his Terran slave killed him with a blaster."

A wide grin splits her face as she turns and studies the forest. "That means she's probably alive out here somewhere."

"Yes. There are several mountains around. I suspect she may be taking shelter in one of the many caves."

Lara stretches up on her toes and wraps her arms around

my neck. "This is wonderful, Markus. We're that much closer to finding one of my people."

Her expression is so full of hope, I dare not speak my worries aloud. Lara's people are not built for this cold weather. I am concerned about the state in which we may find her friend and send a silent prayer to the Creator that we find her alive.

CHAPTER 21

MARKUS

Despite our intense search, we find nothing. Wherever her friend went, the trail must have been covered by snow, for we find no fresh evidence of activity near the downed vessel.

The sun begins to sink low on the horizon, and I cast my glance once more in the direction of the mountain sheltering my warriors. If the storm would let up, they could aid us in our search.

At the very least, I could take Lara there, where she would be safer. Only when I get her to our stronghold will I know for certain the A'kai cannot reach her.

"It will be dark soon."

"We should go back to the shelter."

When we reach the area of the pod, I make sure to scan the forest around us thoroughly before I land, not wanting to give away our position to any enemies. The Lycaons may know where we are, but I also know they would not harm Lara. They recognize I have claimed her by calling her 'mine.'

If Luken had thought otherwise, he would have challenged me. It is their way.

Gently, I land near the shelter. I shift from my draken form and help Lara to the ground. My hair stands up on the back of my neck at the sudden awareness someone, or something, is watching us.

I spin to face the forest as I whisper to Lara. "Get inside the shelter. Now."

"What is—"

"Go," I urge. "Now."

I hear the tap of the control panel behind me and the sound of the door sliding open.

A blur of movement rushes from the shadows, racing toward us. I push Lara into the shelter a moment before the A'kai slams into me, knocking me back against the door.

Pain explodes across the back of my skull, but I force myself to stand. He rushes me again, and we tumble to the ground in a tangled mess of limbs. I shift, and he jumps onto my back.

I flap my wings, lifting into the air, but he rakes his claws across my shoulders, and I fall to the earth once more. I roll onto my back, attempting to crush him, but he's too fast.

Fire ignites in my chest. I open my mouth, releasing a thunderous roar along with a stream of flame and smoke. He screeches when it catches his arm as he spins away.

Another pair of glowing, green eyes catches my attention off to the side, and I spin to face a second A'kai rushing toward me.

I send out another stream of flame, hitting him square in the chest. He releases a feral cry, his body disintegrating before my eyes.

Lightning fast, the other A'kai races toward me again, wrapping his arms around my neck and sinking his canines deep into my flesh. I roar and thrash, the agonizing burn filling me, expanding from the site, as his poison seeps into my veins.

I push him away and watch in horror as the door to the shelter slides open. Lara steps out, brandishing her blaster. He is between her and me, and I don't think she realizes how fast he is. I whip my tail toward him, causing him to stumble and fall.

He recovers quickly and races toward me. A shot rings out, the force of the blast pushing him forward and landing him face-first on the ground. A pool of obsidian blood gathers around his body on the snow.

Fire licks the back of my throat, and I open my mouth, burning him to ash. The A'kai are difficult to kill, and I want to make certain he is dead.

Pain rips through my body as his venom spreads. I start toward Lara but fall to my knees, unable to walk any farther.

She rushes to my side. "Markus? What's wrong?"

"The A'kai," I barely manage as my vision becomes unfocused. "Their bite is toxic to my people. It is paralyzing."

"What can I do?" she asks, her expression frantic. "Tell me."

I open my mouth, but the words seize in my throat. Unable to stay awake any longer, I fall away into the darkened void.

CHAPTER 22

LARA

Markus closes his eyes, his head falling back as he goes unconscious. "Markus? Please, wake up," I beg. Cupping his cheek, I turn his face to me, but he remains still. "Markus, please."

Tears sting my eyes, but I blink them back. I have to get him inside the shelter. I tug at his arm, but he's too heavy, and I cannot move him.

I rush inside the shelter, searching for anything that might help me. Seeing the bed, and the sheet beneath the furs, I quickly gather it and take it outside.

I roll it lengthwise along his side. Using my laser blade to dig out some of the snow and earth beneath him, I shove the sheet up under him as far as I can. Moving to his opposite side, I dig out some more. Then, gripping his shoulder and hip, I manage to roll him just enough to pull the rest of the sheet so it's spread out beneath him.

I grab the two edges up by his head and pull with all my

might. My muscles ache, burning in protest, as I slowly drag him through the snow and ice into the shelter. Once he's inside, I seal the door shut behind us and collapse to the floor at his side.

Rolling onto my back, I pant heavily as I stare up at the snow fall above us. Catching my breath, I stand and manage to pull him to the center of the room.

Only now do I notice the trail of obsidian blood that followed us in, and I remember how the A'kai ripped into his back with his claws.

I grab several furs and use them to prop Markus on his side to clean his wounds.

The emergency kit is still on the side table, and I rifle through the bag until I find the healing gel. Carefully, I squeeze a dollop onto my hand and swallow hard. "I'm sorry," I whisper. "I know this is going to hurt, but I have to do it. All right?"

He doesn't answer, but I didn't expect him to.

When I apply the gel, however, he groans, and I'm glad he's at least aware enough to respond. It gives me hope he's going to wake up soon.

I watch as the gel repairs his flesh, his scales reknitting until I can't even see where the marks were in the first place.

I lay him down on his back and look up at the bed. There's no way I can get him up there. Instead, I pull some furs over and cover us both. Reaching up, I press a tender kiss to his lips then rest my forehead to his as I cup his cheek. "Please, wake up soon, Markus. I want to see your smile and your gorgeous violet eyes, my love."

My love.

The words escape my lips unfiltered, and I realize they are true. I *do* love him. I was too afraid before, to admit my feelings for him. But now, I wish I'd told him sooner.

I nestle down beside him, resting my head on his shoulder and my hand on his chest. The steady rhythm of his heart beating beneath my palm reassures me he is still alive. Closing my eyes, I allow myself to fall away into a fitful sleep.

CHAPTER 23

MARKUS

When I wake, Lara is lying beside me, her head on my shoulder, arm draped across my chest. I do not know how long I've been unconscious, but I no longer feel the poisonous venom of the A'kai in my veins.

I gently nuzzle her hair, breathing deep of her delicate scent, so relieved she is alive and well, here beside me. Before I passed out, I worried there might be more A'kai lurking nearby, ready to attack the moment I went unconscious.

Gently, I skim the tip of my nose alongside hers, across her jaw and then down the elegant curve of her neck. A low rumbling growl vibrates my chest and her eyes snap open.

"Markus?" She smiles. "You're awake."

She presses her mouth to mine in a Terran kiss. My heart hammers as she darts her small tongue out to trace the seam of my lips. I wrap my arms and wings around her, pulling her close.

A voice comes over the computer, and I immediately

recognize it as Rokan. "Commander Markus, are you out there?"

I groan as I force myself to pull away from Lara. While I am glad to be able to reach him finally, I curse Rokan's timing. I tap the screen, and his face appears a moment later. He smiles. "The storm has cleared. Did you find what you were searching for?"

"Yes, I did"—I turn my head quickly toward Lara and back again to the viewer—"and I have something important to share with all of you."

"What is it?"

"It would be best if I show you. I will return shortly. Look for me along the wall."

He dips his chin in agreement. "We will, Commander."

I turn to Lara. "The storm has cleared. We should return."

She agrees, but I note the hesitance in her features.

I take her hand. "What is wrong?"

Her eyes meet mine. "I look like a V'loryn. Your people don't like them."

I understand the source of her concern, so I move to reassure her. "My warriors will accept you, Lara. I know this without doubt. You have nothing to worry about. I swear it to the Creator."

CHAPTER 24

MARKUS

Despite the fact the storm has cleared, the air has grown colder. Thick, heavy snow is beginning to fall. Another storm is coming this way, and I know we cannot hesitate to leave. It could worsen, if we linger, blocking our path once more.

It worries me how cold Lara appears.

I pull back just enough to meet her eyes evenly. "I will shift and pick you up. It will be warmer for you if I carry you in my hand."

"All right. I'm ready."

I step back and tighten the cinch once more on her furs, making sure they are layered close to her body for warmth.

I move back farther and shift forms. Without hesitation, I wrap my clawed hand around her, making sure to hold her close to my chest as I lift off into the wind and back into the storm.

The air grows colder still, and snow swirls thick around us, making it difficult to see. The wind is billowing, threatening to slam me into the side of a nearby mountain. I flap my wings furiously and press on. We have to get through this. There is no turning back now.

The dark clouds overhead block out all light from the sun, making it appear as though it were night instead of midday. Her small form shivers in my grasp, steeling my resolve.

Hope flares in my chest when I notice the light in the distance and the vague outline of the mountain that is our home—our fortress. *"We are almost there, Lara."*

"Thank goodness." Her mind speaks back to me for the first time, and I marvel once more at our connection. Only Ashaya—fated mates—are able to speak to each other in this way. I have not yet talked to her about this, and I do not even know how to bring it up. I only know that I must. And soon.

I must ask her again about her kiss. I am curious to understand. I wonder if it is how her people claim their mates.

I think about my warriors, waiting for my return. They will be surprised to see her, even more shocked when they find out she is my Ashaya.

The mere thought of being around other males—even my own warriors—is already beginning to affect me. Intense possessiveness overcomes me as I hold her close to my chest. When the outer ice wall of the fort comes into view, I see Rokan standing at his post, staring out at the forest around him.

The moment he notices us, he turns and calls out to the others. Although I had already spoken to them and they knew I was not dead, it is like any time one of us has been stranded from our stronghold: the return is always a relief.

I circle just above the base of the mountain, near the main cavern entrance, and gently touch down. Rokan flies over to me, a bright smile on his face, as the rest of our warriors gather around.

Carefully, I uncurl my hand and lower Lara to the ground. I shift a moment later and wrap a possessive arm around her as the warriors stare, dumbfounded.

"This is Lara."

Rokan blinks several times, a question in his eyes. But the moment his eyes meets hers, he bows his head in respect. "I am Rokan."

"I am Siran"—he bows humbly to her—"I am a Healer. Would you like to me assess you?"

She smiles. "Thank you, but aside from being cold, I feel fine."

I observe the shock in each warrior's face as she smiles at them. They probably believe she is V'loryn, and everyone knows they do not express emotion. I inspect their faces, curious. "Lara is Terran."

Siran frowns. "Terran? I have never heard of this race."

"That's because her world is part of an uncharted system."

"But how did—"

"My crew and I were taken while we were in stasis sleep, traveling between planets in our system," she explains. "When I woke up, I was on a slave ship."

Rokan steps forward. "Where is your home world?"

"I don't know. Our people have never left our system."

His eyes widen.

I step forward. "There are more of Lara's people here on the planet. They were on an A'kai slave ship that got caught by the wormhole. They ejected in escape pods, just before the ship exploded, and crash-landed here."

"How many of you were there?" Rokan asks.

"There were at least twenty of us... probably more," she replies. "But, there were many more A'kai."

Siran gasps at the mention of more A'kai.

Rokan's head snaps to me. "We will have to increase our defense patrols."

"And we must search for Lara's people. The V'loryns and the Lycaons are already aware of their presence. We saw Commander Vorek and Luken while we were in the forest."

"Have they found any—"

I shake my head. "The Lycaons are tracking the A'kai, trying to determine their location."

Silence settles in the space between us before Siran turns his attention to Lara. "Because we will be searching for your people, I would ask you please allow me to scan you so I might familiarize myself with your anatomy. I wish to be prepared to treat any injured who may come to us."

"All right. When would you like to begin?"

"How about after you are rested?"

She gives him a warm smile.

I turn to her. "Are you hungry? Thirsty?"

She shakes her head. "I just a bit tired. That's all."

I look to my warriors. Each of them gives me a subtle nod. I lead her into the cave entrance. "You may stay in my quarters. But first, I will show you around so you might familiarize yourself with the tunnels connecting the mountain's structures. Come. I will show you."

CHAPTER 25

LARA

As Markus leads me deeper into the mountain, the air is surprisingly crisp and clean. Not damp and earthy like I'd thought it might be. It's dark in here. There are lights spaced out along the tunnels, but there is quite a bit of distance between them. I suppose that's because Markus's people have better night vision than mine do. I slow my steps, afraid I might accidentally run into something.

"Markus? I'm having trouble seeing clearly in the dark."

He stops and turns to me. "I will help guide you, Lara. And I will speak with our engineers about adding more light to the tunnels. We will need it when we find more of your people."

"Thank you." I smile. He's so thoughtful, and his people were very welcoming. I'd thought I would be nervous to meet them, but they are friendly and completely put my mind at ease.

From what I can see, the walls and floor are smooth,

slate-gray-and-black stone. Whatever process they used to create these tunnels was such that there are no sharp edges, not even along the ceilings, and the spaces carved out are very large. Big enough for five Mosaurans to walk side by side and tall enough that, if not for the darkness, I certainly wouldn't feel closed in, wandering through these areas.

Every now and then, a larger cavern opens up, surrounded by several tunnels leading away from it in various directions. As a navigator, I understand how important it is to keep one's bearings. So, I make sure to keep a mental note of how many turns we take and in what directions.

When we reach Markus's quarters, I'm surprised he has a metal door at the entrance. As if sensing my question, he turns to me. "We have scavenged much from both our ship and others we've found on this planet, including technology."

"The lights," I say more to myself than to him.

"Yes. Our ship is no longer space-worthy, so we use the power cells to control the lights, and our engineers have created a system to regulate the temperature, as well as water and waste, throughout the mountain's structure."

My mouth drifts open. "That's incredible."

When he opens the door, my jaw drops even farther.

A large bed sits against the far wall, piled high with white furs. There is a sofa along another wall, and in an adjoining room, there is a cleansing room of sorts. A sunken pool in the center of the floor, with steam rising from the surface, draws my attention. "Is that warm water?"

"Yes. There is a natural spring that our engineers tapped into. They found a way to use it to provide cleansing rooms and fresh water for this entire complex."

As he goes over the various technologies they've incorporated, I struggle to imagine the level of tech it takes to do all these things. Terrans certainly aren't as advanced as his appear to be.

He gestures to a wall panel similar to the one we used in the shelter. "This is set up with a comm system. You can use it to contact me, if you need anything."

I start to ask where he's going, but then I remember he's the Commander, and he, of course, has responsibilities, now that we're back.

Things were left off kind of awkward back at the shelter, and I don't want him to leave just yet. I was hoping we could talk some more, but maybe we can, when he comes back.

"I will return to you as soon as I can," he says.

"All right."

When he leaves, I peel off my several layers of fur and submerge myself into the warm pool. The water is so relaxing, it melts away all my tension.

After I'm finished, I dry off and re-dress. I don't need as many layers of fur here in the mountain complex, so I simply put on a few, instead of everything I was wearing earlier. I decide to go exploring to familiarize myself with this place while Markus is gone.

CHAPTER 26

MARKUS

I leave Lara alone in my quarters as I go to speak with my warriors. We must form a plan, and it must be done soon. Lara's people are still out there, and we cannot leave them in the hands of the A'kai. That is a fate worse than death.

When I reach the outside, almost everyone is already waiting. Rokan flies down from the wall to join us. He steps forward. "Her people... they appear so much like the V'loryns. It is strange, is it not?"

"Yes. Commander Vorek also thought she was one of theirs, when we saw him."

Rokan darts a glance at the wall. "We should double the watch. And we must begin searching for the rest of her people immediately. We cannot leave them in the hands of the A'kai."

The others nod in agreement, and I have never been more proud of my warriors. Despite the fact Lara and her people look so much like the V'loryn's—a race we do not trust—they have already accepted her and are ready to find the others and protect them.

Rokan's gaze meets mine, and I note the hesitation in his expression as he steps forward. "Forgive me, Commander, but... the female. You seem very protective of her. Is she your mate?"

I survey my warriors. Drawing in a deep breath, I prepare to give them my truth, no matter how strange it may seem. "She is my Ashaya."

Their eyes go wide, and everyone falls silent.

Siran cocks his head to the side. "But she is not Mosauran. No one has ever found his Ashaya outside of our race. Are you certain?"

Even though I understand why he asks this, I bristle slightly at his doubt. "When I carry her in my draken form, she can hear my thoughts, and I can hear hers."

Rokan inhales sharply. "Then, it *is* truth."

"Yes. I felt the pull to her the moment her eyes met mine. I rescued her from an A'kai who held her in a deadly embrace as he drank of her blood." I pause. "She is a gift from the Creator. Of this, I am certain. We must find and rescue her people and bring them back to the safety of our mountain."

Rokan's eyes fill with hope. "If Lara is your Ashaya, the others may be—"

"Fated to one of us." Siran finishes his sentence.

It is the highest blessing a warrior can receive from the Creator—to be blessed with a fated bond. "Yes. This could be true," I tell them. "I will need volunteers to search for her people. We will leave at dawn tomorrow."

"Yes, Commander," they reply in unison.

With that, I turn and head back into the mountain, eager to check in on Lara. I have not told her she is my Ashaya, and I do not know how to. But I know I must try.

When I reach my quarters, I find them empty. Several of her furs are folded on the floor near the bathing pool, but she is not here. A feeling of uneasiness arises, but I quickly relax, remembering she is not in any danger here. My warriors guard the mountain and the wall. No A'kai can breach our defenses.

Stepping out into the tunnel, my nostrils flare, detecting her delicate scent. I follow it through the corridor until I reach our crashed ship. It is half buried in the mountain, and our tunnels connect to its entrance while the viewscreen looks out on the wall and the forest beyond.

Stepping inside, the sound of Lara's laughter draws my attention. My head snaps toward her, and jealousy flares brightly within at finding her lying on the exam table and speaking with Healer Siran, seeing him smile at her in return while running the med scanner over her frame.

He studies the readout with a slight frown.

"What do you think?" she asks. "Am I going to live?"

Panic envelopes me, and I rush toward her. "What is wrong? Are you ill?" I turn to Siran. "Is she all right?"

She takes my hand, squeezing it gently. "I was just joking with him, Markus. I feel fine."

Siran purses his lips. "She is healthy, as far as I can tell." He narrows his eyes as he studies the screen. "But there is something at the base of her neck. A... tracker of some sort."

Lara's eyes widen as he enlarges it on the screen.

"If you would, please turn over."

She turns onto her side, but I am aware she does not release my hand. Her palm grips mine a bit tighter with worry.

"I must unfasten your clothing to get a better look. Is that all right?" Siran asks.

She nods but I note her brow is furrowed, accentuating her concern.

Gently, I brush the hair back from her face, trying to soothe her.

Siran growls under his breath.

"What is it?" I ask, trying but failing to hide the alarm in my voice.

"The A'kai placed a tracker near her spine. It will be difficult to remove, but not impossible."

I move around the table, and my jaw drops at seeing the crisscross pattern of scars across her back. The thick, jagged red marks are so many.

How did she live through this?

I had felt them when I held her the other night, but I had no idea how severe they were. I struggle to push down my rage. I will tear the A'kai limb from limb for what they have done to her. These are slave markings, created with a silic-acid tipped blade.

No med repair unit can mend these. They are meant to be permanent. Usually, the Zovians and Anguis make these, but in her marred flesh, I recognize the A'kai glyphs.

Blood breeder.

Siran's eyes are wide as they meet mine. The A'kai not only wanted her people for their blood, they also wanted to breed them.

"We have to find the others," I tell him. "Quickly."

"Yes."

"Can you remove the tracker now?" Lara asks. "I don't want them to be able to find me."

I take her hand. "Even if they tracked you here, you are safe, Lara. Our warriors will protect you. None can breach our defenses."

"I'd still like it removed."

I look to Siran, and he dips his head. "We can do it now, but I must sedate you."

Fear fills her eyes. "Do you have to?"

"Yes. It is a delicate procedure, and I cannot risk you moving."

She looks to me. "Will you stay with me?"

I would have stayed, even if she had not asked. "Always."

She gives me a faint smile and turns back to Siran. "Please. Take this tracker out of me."

"As you wish."

He injects her with a sedative, and I watch as her eyelids flutter open and closed before she falls asleep. I sit beside her bed, holding her hand in mine.

Siran's eyes meet mine over the table. "She will be fine, Commander."

Despite his words, I cannot help but worry. Rubbing the pad of my thumb across her knuckles, I am struck again by her delicate bones. She is fragile and, yet, her strength of will and her bravery rival that of my people.

Sensing my thoughts, Siran speaks. "She is very brave, your Ashaya."

Unable to speak through my fear, I nod.

As he cuts into her flesh, I grit my teeth. "I cannot believe she survived such torture," I tell him, thinking of the many marks across her flesh.

"The A'kai are as cruel as they are ruthless. Why would they abuse the very females they meant to breed?"

"I do not understand. I only know when we find them, we will kill them all."

"Agreed," he says.

When he is done removing the tracking chip, he places it in a metal container. I arch a brow. "Should it not be destroyed?"

"If the other Terrans have trackers like this, perhaps I can isolate the signals. We can then use this to determine where they are."

Siran has always had a brilliant mind. It is why I

requested him as the Healer of our vessel. I have infallibly respected him since our time together in training. "Excellent plan, Siran."

He dips his chin. "Thank you, Markus."

Carefully, he reseals Lara's wound and looks to me. "I will stay here with her until she awakens."

"No. I will take her back to my quarters."

I expect him to argue, but he does not. He glances at our joined hands. "She trusts you. Does she also recognize the bond between you?"

I shake my head. "I do not believe so." I sigh. "I will speak with her about it when she awakens. But I would ask one more thing of you."

"What is it?"

"Will you watch over her while I am gone to search for her people?"

"Of course, Commander. It would be my honor."

When I take Lara to my quarters, I lay her gently on the bed, beneath a few layers of fur to keep her warm. As I pull away, she makes a small sound of protest, and I stop.

"Stay," she whispers.

"Lara?"

When she doesn't respond, I know she is still sleeping, but I am reluctant to let go of her. Gently, I settle in the bed beside her, and she turns onto her side, curling into my chest.

Carefully, I wrap my arms and wings around her smaller form, listening intently to the soft sound of her breathing as she sleeps. I cannot deny that I love holding her like this. I wish that I could hold her forever.

CHAPTER 27

LARA

When I wake, I'm pressed against Markus's chest, his arms and wings wrapped protectively around me. I'm very warm and feel so safe in his arms, I want to just stay here forever. I've fallen for Markus, but I don't know how he feels about me.

I pull back and find his violet eyes studying me. My cheeks heat as our eyes lock.

A faint smile tips my lips. "You stayed with me?"

He nods. "When I laid you down on the bed, you refused to let me go. But if you are uncomfortable, I will—"

"It's fine," I tell him. "I like sleeping like this… with you."

The green marks of his cheeks flush even darker as his eyes search mine. "You do?"

I reach out and touch the sharp ridge of his brow, tracing my fingers along the rough edge. "Yes."

"There is something I must tell you, Lara."

"What is it?"

His expression is so solemn it worries me. Perhaps, I'm

too familiar with him, and he doesn't know how to tell me he doesn't feel that way about me. I look away, insecure and unsure of what to do.

"I'm sorry I kissed you, Markus."

"What does a kiss mean to your people?" He places two fingers up under my chin and locks eyes with me, taking my breath away. "Does it mean you want me? Because I have desired you as mine from the moment we first met. You are my Ashaya, and I long to claim you more than anything."

My mouth drifts open. "What is 'Ashaya'?"

He leans in and skims the tip of his nose alongside mine. "Ashaya means 'fated one,' in the ancient tongue. You are my Ashaya, Lara. And I feel it here." He takes my hand and places it on his chest. "You are my heart, and I want nothing more than to claim you."

Cautiously, I lean in and gently brush my lips to his as he whispers against them. "If this is how your people claim their mates, then give me another kiss, Lara, for I wish to be yours."

I open my mouth, and a soft moan escapes me the moment his tongue strokes against mine. The ridges of his tongue feel amazing as he takes control of the kiss, leaving me breathless and panting when he finally pulls away.

I trace my hand down the hard planes of muscle lining his abdomen and chest. Softly, I bite my lower lip as I explore him.

CHAPTER 28

MARKUS

Her tongue traces along the seam of my lips, asking for entrance. When I open my mouth, her tongue finds mine, curling around it.

I wrap my arms and wings around her, pulling her so close there is no space between us. My stav lengthens and extends from my body, seeking the heat of her center. She moans into my mouth as I roll my hips against hers.

I trace my hand down the length of her body, and she arches into my touch. "Show me how to touch you," I breathe against her lips. "I want only to give you pleasure, my beautiful Ashaya."

She pulls back just enough to remove the fur covering her body. I am in awe as I study her form, silently admiring the sensuous mounds of her breasts, the slight dip of her waist, and the gentle flare of her hips. "You are perfect," I whisper.

She looks down my body to my stav, hard and erect. She reaches out, and I inhale sharply as she traces the ridges along my length with her fingers.

Liquid beads on the tip in anticipation of joining my body to hers. Every muscle in my body is tense in a struggle to maintain my control. Everything inside me wants to claim her. To roll her beneath me, giving her my mark as I fill her with my seed.

"Tell me how you long to be touched," I rasp.

She leans in and presses her lips to mine again. Her tongue finds mine, deepening our kiss. She takes my hand and places my palm over the globe of her breast. Her body is so soft and giving. I brush my thumb over the peak, and it hardens into a small bead.

I lean down and close my mouth over her breast, laving my tongue across the tip. She threads her fingers through my hair, holding me close. My nostrils flare and need burns through me like fire as the scent of her arousal grows thick in the air.

Pressing a series of tender kisses down the length of her body, I run my hand along her inner thigh, opening her to my gaze. I lift my eyes to hers to find her watching me intently. "I want to taste you."

She nods, and I dip my head between her thighs. I drag my tongue through her already slick folds and close my eyes as I relish her taste. Her nectar is exquisite. She arches against me and moans as my tongue travels over a sensitive bead of flesh at the top.

I concentrate my attention on the small bundle of nerves, savoring the light moans that escape her lips and the way she grips my hair. Her entire body lights up with pleasure when I tease my tongue over the softly hooded flesh.

Her heels dig into my shoulders, and a low growl vibrates my chest as she writhes beneath my attentions.

I band my arm over her waist, holding her in place, continuing to lap at her folds. Her entire body goes taut, and she cries out my name as she finds her release.

I move up her body, and she kisses me long and deep.

The scent of her need is growing stronger, driving me mad with desire. I'm consumed with the desire to possess her, to claim her. I want to sheathe myself deep inside her warm, wet heat and take her over and over again, filling her with my seed.

But, I am afraid as soon as the realization hits me. Her scent is stronger now, and although we are different species, I suspect it is her fertile peak. And I fear it has triggered my mating heat.

She reaches for me, but I grip her wrist, stopping her. "We must stop," I rasp.

"Why?"

"My mating heat approaches. I worry that if I take you now, I may hurt you."

She cups his cheek. "You won't hurt me, Markus."

In her eyes, I see the truth. She believes this. She trusts me. She does not realize how much stronger I am than her.

I move off to the side and sit up on the edge of the bed, running a hand roughly through my hair and standing. "I must go."

"What? Where are you going?"

"To the Healer. I must ask him to inject me with a suppressant."

She reaches for me, but I pull away. "Please, Lara. I do not trust myself right now. I am barely able to maintain my control. I must go. I will return as soon as I can."

Before she can say anything else, I force myself to leave. I cannot risk remaining with her any longer. Not until after I visit Siran.

CHAPTER 29

MARKUS

I head straight to the Med Center of the ship, relieved when Siran greets me at the door. His face falls when he notices my expression. "What is wrong?"

"My mating heat," I explain. "I need a suppressant."

He blinks at me. "She triggered your mating heat?"

Need burns through me like fire. I clench my fists at my side as I grit through my teeth. "Yes," I growl in frustration. "Now, where is the suppressant? I need it."

He blinks several times and rushes to one of the nearby cabinets. He quickly fills the injector and presses it to my neck. The slight click is followed by the low hissing sound of the medicine entering my system.

Even now, it takes everything inside me not to race back to her, pin her against the wall and—

I squeeze my eyes shut, ashamed of myself for even thinking of taking her that roughly.

I jerk my head up, leering at Siran. "How long will it take to work?"

"Give it a few minutes."

I turn from him, slamming my fist down on the table, the indentation remaining in the metal after I lift my hand away. Lowering my eyes, I draw in several deep breaths, attempting to calm the fire in my veins.

After a moment, I feel my desire beginning to ebb. I sit back on the table and drop my head in my hands as the medicine slowly begins to work.

"This is interesting," Siran mumbles to himself.

"What?" I ask, unable to hide the irritation in my voice as I wait for the medicine to take full effect.

"She is fertile."

"Of course, she is," I snap. "Why else would I be responding to her in this way?"

He purses his lips. "What I mean is... she is not only fertile, she is compatible with our species."

My head jerks up. "What? How is this possible?"

"Their biology... it is... highly adaptable it seems."

I frown. "You are certain?"

"Yes. Fledglings may be possible between you. It may require some medical intervention, but... it is not outside the realm of possibility."

Fledglings.

I never thought this might happen with Lara. We are two different species, yet, the Creator has blessed me with not only the most perfect mate, but also one I may create life with.

Happiness fills me at the thought of someday having a family with my Ashaya.

"The suppressant should see you through your mating heat without problem," he adds. "It should not be difficult, now, if you wish to return to her."

Without hesitation, I make my way back to Lara.

When I reach my quarters, I find her asleep beneath the

furs. I sit on the edge of the bed, studying her as she sleeps. Tenderly, I comb the hair back from her face. Her eyelids flutter open, and she smiles at me.

She takes my hand and threads her fingers through mine. "Come to bed," she whispers.

She rolls onto her side and pulls me with her. I nestle beneath the covers, beside her, curling my body protectively around hers, pressing a kiss to her temple. "I am sorry... for earlier."

She turns in my arms and cups my cheek. "It's all right, my love. You have nothing to be sorry for."

I gently nuzzle her temple. "I must leave in the morning. We are going to search for your people. I will be gone for a few days, but Siran will watch over you while—"

"I'm not staying behind."

"It is safer for you to remain here, Lara."

"*No*. I can't stay here. Not while my friends are out there missing, Markus. I have to help find them."

"We can—"

"They don't know you. They might be afraid of your people. With all we've suffered, I need to be there when you find them. To help reassure them they are safe." She cups my cheek. "Not only that but... I don't want to be apart from you, Markus."

What she says about her people makes sense, but I do not want her in harm's way. As much as I want her with me, I do not want her in danger. Not now that I've already gotten her safely here, to our territory.

"Please, Lara. I want you to stay here, where I know you are safe from the A'kai."

She takes my hand. "And you think I won't be worried about *you* while you're gone?"

I frown. "Are you suggesting I am weak?"

I wait anxiously for her answer. If a female Mosauran

made a statement like this, it would mean she did not believe I am strong, and she certainly would not consider me as a potential mate.

"That's not what I'm saying," she counters. "I just... I want to be with you. Together, we can search, and we can protect each other while we try to find my friends."

"No. I will not risk you being caught by the A'kai."

She pushes away from me. "It's my decision. Not yours."

"Please." I drop my forehead to hers. "I do not want to argue with you. I am only trying to keep you safe."

"Fine." She sighs. "We won't argue."

Relief fills me at her words as she settles back against me. I wrap my wings around her, and she snuggles into my chest. "I will return to you as soon as I can, Lara."

She says nothing, and her silence worries me, but I am hesitant to press her. I know she is upset, but this is for the best. I will not have her in danger. Not now that I have brought her to the safety of our territory. She is too precious to me, and I will not risk losing her.

CHAPTER 30

MARKUS

When I wake in the morning, Lara is not in my arms, nor is she even in the bed. I sit up as a wash of fear comes over me.

The doors to the cleansing room slide open and she steps out, wearing only a towel.

She smiles at me and I move toward her, gathering her up in my arms. Gently, I nuzzle her hair and then give her a tender kiss. "I will return to you as soon as I can, Lara."

"I'm not staying behind. I'm going with you."

"It is dangerous, my Ashaya."

"That's why I want to go with you. To help watch your back, Markus."

Her concern touches my heart, but I cannot bear the thought of her in danger. The A'kai are still out there and we do not know how many of them survived the crash.

"I want you to stay here, where it is safe."

"And *I* want to stay with you," she counters. "Besides,

they're my people, Markus. They don't know you. If I'm there, they won't be afraid."

I'm still trying to convince her to stay as we walk out of the mountain and toward the ice wall.

Rokan walks over to us, smiling as he approaches. "Are you ready to leave, Commander?"

"Yes."

I turn back to Lara. "Healer Siran will—"

"I'm going with you," she insists for, at least, the tenth time.

"Lara, I—"

"If you won't fly me, I'll ask Rokan."

Jealousy flares deep inside me. My eyes snap to Rokan and narrow.

His lips part on a breath. "Commander, I—"

She places her hand on my chest. "I don't want to be apart from you, and I want to help search for my people. Wouldn't you feel the same?"

Her words give me pause. Drawing in a deep breath, I lock eyes with her. "Fine."

She gives me a beaming smile, stretching up on her toes and wrapping her arms around my neck before pressing her lips to mine in a tender kiss. "Thank you."

Rokan's attention is heavy on us. He is the youngest among us, but it is no secret that he has longed for a mate these past five cycles. Every time I think of him, I worry that my mistake may have cost him a chance at ever finding a mate.

I saw the hope that flared in his eyes when he learned that Lara is my Ashaya. He is eager to find her people, hoping his Ashaya may be among them as well. He is probably wondering at Lara's Terran kiss. Our people do not do this, and I'm certain it must be a strange sight to him.

He gapes at me a moment before snapping to attention. "Gather the warriors," I order. "We are leaving now."

We each shift into draken form. They watch with curious stares as I wrap my tail around Lara's waist and settle her onto my back between my shoulders before lifting off to begin the search.

We take to the skies, flying in formation for a while before finally splitting off in different directions.

"Where are they going?" Lara asks.

"Each of us will be staying at a different outpost while we search. By spreading out, we can cover more ground while we look for your people."

"Where are we going?"

"Back to the shelter where we stayed before."

She must be satisfied with my answer, because she flattens herself against my back.

"When we get there, I will seek out Luken and Dakor to see if they have found any of your people or the A'kai."

As soon as we get close to the shelter, my nostrils flare as I scent the Lycaons, their stench causing me to wrinkle my nose in disgust.

"The Lycaons have been here recently."

"Can you tell if anyone else has been here?"

"No." What I do not tell her is, the A'kai mask their scent so well, I would probably be unable to detect them.

Carefully, I circle a few times before landing just outside the shelter. I make sure to watch the forest for any signs of movement. Once I'm satisfied we are alone, I shift from my draken form, and we enter the hidden shelter.

I draw in a deep breath as we enter, scenting for any sign others have been here, but I sense nothing. This is good. I am always worried each time I come here that one of the other races will have discovered this hidden structure. So far, it has remained a secret from all but the Lycaons.

Snow is falling steadily outside, for which I am thankful. It will cover our tracks into the shelter pod, concealing we are here.

Lara sits on the bed and turns to me. "Where do the others stay? Other places like this?"

I shake my head. "We have a few more of these. There are also other locations we use in caves high up in the mountains, to make it hard for any but the Aerilon to reach us."

Her expression appears distraught, and I suddenly realize why. She is worried for her friends—concerned they may be found by one of the others and mistreated. So, I quickly move to reassure her.

"Of all the others, it is only the A'kai who condone slavery. The rest are like my people. On this, we can at least agree." I open my mouth to speak further when a low howl draws my attention outside, followed quickly by a chorus of others joining it.

"Are those the Lycaons?"

"Yes." I stand. "I will be back. I must speak with them. See if they've found any of your people."

When I start for the door, she calls out, stopping me abruptly. "Wait. I want to go with you."

I frown. "You are safer here."

"You said the other races here are against slavery. Do you really think they would harm me?"

With tension in my face, I shake my head.

Lara stands from the bed and begins wrapping the furs all around her. "Then, I'm coming with you, Markus."

CHAPTER 31

MARKUS

I know the Lycaons would not hurt Lara, but they may try to take her from me. She is one of the only females on this planet, and the Lycaons are fiercely protective of them—regardless of species. It is instinct for their pack to protect females and young.

It occurs to me I could keep arguing for Lara to stay here, but I doubt she will listen, so I do not even try. I give her a reluctant nod. "Stay close to me."

"All right."

Together, we exit the pod and head in the direction of the sound. Movement draws my attention, and I spin to face it, only to be met by a pair of orange, glowing eyes. "Luken," I call.

He steps out of the shadows and dips his head in slight greeting. "Markus"—he looks then nods toward her—"Lara."

"What have you found?"

His expression turns grim. "Come. I will show you."

Lara takes my hand, threading her fingers through mine

as we follow after him. Several of his brethren, in their two-legged form, stand in a circle, each staring down at something on the ground.

A scent touches my nostrils, and I straighten, the realization of what it is hitting me with full force. It is the scent of a Terran.

Sensing our approach, the Lycaons turn their heads to us, their eyes going straight to Lara.

"What are they—"

I stop, tugging on her hand, halting her progress. "Wait, Lara. Let me go look."

She frowns. "Why?"

She shoots a glance back to the Lycaons and rips her hand from mine, running toward them.

I chase after her. "Lara, wait!"

She pushes between them, and her jaw goes slack, eyes wide in horror as she stares down at something in the snow. As soon as I reach her, I notice a hand, delicate and fine-boned like hers, sticking up out of the snow. "No," she whispers under her breath.

She drops her knees and digs furiously, trying to uncover the horror that lies beneath.

A female's face is revealed: her eyes are closed as though asleep, lips and skin a light shade of gray, and she has short blonde hair.

Bile rises in my throat. That could so easily have been my Ashaya if I had not found her when I did.

"Beth!" Lara touches her face. A mournful wail escapes her as she takes the woman's hand and cries her anguish to the sky. I scan the deceased female, observing the two puncture wounds on the side of her neck. Beside me, Luken lets out a muffled growl, having noticed, too. "The A'kai," he snarls. "They killed her."

I kneel beside Lara as her entire body shudders with sobs.

She turns to me and buries her face in my chest. "They murdered her, Markus," her voice quavers. "They drank her blood."

I gather her in my arms and hold her close. "We will find them, Lara, and we will make them pay."

"The A'kai will answer for this," Luken offers. "We will show them no mercy in the hunt." He kneels beside us and places a hand on her shoulder.

"Thank you," she barely manages. She turns a tear-filled gaze to me. "We cannot just leave her like this."

"We won't, Lara."

Luken glances over his shoulder at his pack. "Gather the wood," he instructs.

It doesn't take the Lycaons long to stack the wood. Together, we lift Lara's friend from the snow and gently place her atop the pyre. Luken looks to me and hands me a branch.

I shift into draken form, open my mouth, and set it aflame before handing it back to him.

He meets Lara's eyes evenly as he presents it to her. "We will stand watch with you, and we will call to the Creator of the Moon and the Stars to ask her to welcome your friend into the life beyond this one."

"Thank you," she whispers.

She takes the torch from his hand and walks to the pyre. Carefully, she places it up under the wood and steps back as the flames catch and begin to burn.

I wrap my arm and wing around her, holding her close. The Lycaons shift form, lift their heads, and cry out their mournful howls to the Great Creator of all things.

When the fire dies down, and only ash remains, Luken shifts forms again and walks over to me, his glowing, orange eyes meeting mine evenly. "Our people have never been friends, but upon one thing we can agree: the A'kai must be killed and the Terrans rescued. Our pack will join yours in the hunt, warrior of Mosaura."

I dip my chin in a firm nod. "Thank you."

He turns to his pack, his commanding stare traveling over each of them. "We join the Mosaurans in the hunt for the ones who did this. Together, we will find them and make them pay for their crimes. We will save the Terrans and reunite them with their people."

His eyes meet mine, and he extends his arm. I clasp my hand around his forearm, and he returns the gesture. "Good hunting, Commander Markus of the Mosauran Empire."

"Good hunting, Luken, Alpha of the Lycaon Clan."

He dips his chin affirmatively and turns back to his people. Lara and I watch as he shifts once more into his four-legged form and joins his pack, racing through the woods.

CHAPTER 32

LARA

Markus and I walk in silence back to the shelter. Snow falls steadily, covering our tracks. I'm numb as we enter. Markus helps me peel away the outer layers of my clothing until I'm left only in one of the furs.

The image of Beth's face, her eyes closed, replays in my mind. I can't believe she is dead.

Markus guides me to the bed and carefully tucks me in beneath the layers of furs. "Rest," he whispers.

I take his hand and lift my gaze to him. "Stay with me."

He nods. "I must inform the others of what we have found, first. Then, I will join you."

I listen as he relays the information to Rokan and asks that he spread the message among their people.

"Of course, Commander," Rokan's voice comes over the speaker. He pauses. "Will you please convey my sorrow to Lara about the passing of her friend. Tell her I will say a special prayer to the Creator for her."

Tears sting my eyes. Markus's people are so kind. I turn, and Markus's watchful attention greets me. He gives me a pained smile. "I will, Rokan," he says. "I would ask you also go to the V'loryns and the Aerilon. Make them aware of what we have discovered, and inquire whether they have rescued anyone."

"I will, Commander."

Markus cuts off the screen and slips into the bed beside me, beneath the blankets.

I curl into him, burying my face in his chest. "That would have been me, if you hadn't saved me from the A'kai," I whisper the words before I even realize I've spoken them aloud.

He wraps his wings around me, holding me close as he gently nuzzles my temple.

"I can't stop thinking about the others. What if they're all—"

"No," he says. "Do not give up hope, Lara. All of us are searching for them now. The V'loryns, the Lycaons and, I'm sure, the Aerilon, since Commander Vorek would have told them about our meeting."

"It's not just us, Markus. Before the A'kai bought me... I saw some of my people being traded in the slave markets."

Tears stream down my cheeks as silent sobs move through me. Markus holds me as I cry, whispering soothing words of comfort in my ear, his body wrapped protectively around mine.

After a while, my eyelids grow heavy, and I close my eyes, allowing myself to drift away into oblivion.

CHAPTER 33

LARA

It's been two days, and we still haven't found any sign of my friends. The problem is, they could be anywhere. And even though Siran is trying to use my tracker to locate their signals, he hasn't had any luck.

Rokan and a few of the other engineers are trying to modify their equipment to track the A'kai signals, but they haven't been successful.

As the sun sets low on the horizon, Markus and I make our way back to the shelter. He's been quiet most of the day, and I wonder if it's worry or something else on his mind. I open my mouth to speak, but the moment we step inside, he pulls me into his arms and seals his mouth over mine in a claiming kiss, stealing the breath from my lungs.

He rips his mouth from mine. Panting heavily, he clenches his jaw and lowers his head. "My mating heat... the suppressant has worn off. Your scent," he whispers. "It is driving me mad. I tried to ignore it. But I cannot."

"Markus, it's all right." I reach for him, but he pulls away.

He moves to the console. "I must contact Rokan. I will tell him to come stay with you while I leave. I cannot be near you during this time. Not while I—"

"No," I state firmly. "You don't have to leave."

"Lara, I—"

"Shav-rhokan."

He stills. His gaze meets mine, full of desire. He stalks toward me, backing me into the wall, his violet eyes staring deep into mine. His voice is a deep, rumbling growl as he speaks. "You do not know what you are saying."

"Yes, I do." I tip my face up to his. "I am challenging you to the shav-rhokan."

The muscles tick along his jaw. "You are certain?"

Breathless with anticipation, I barely manage to nod.

His nostrils flare, and he leans in, skimming the tip of his nose from my temple to my jaw and down the curve of my neck and shoulder. A deep growl resounds in his chest. "I can scent your need, my Ashaya."

He moves close, pressing his body against mine. My pulse pounds as I feel the hard press of his length between us. He wraps his arms around me and tunnels his fingers through my long hair. Gripping the strands, he tilts my head to one side exposing the column of my neck.

His grasp is firm, but it doesn't scare me. This is Markus. I trust him completely.

My heart races as he scents along the curve of my neck and shoulder. My every nerve ending is on fire at his touch. "Do you accept me as yours, Lara?" His warm breath whispers across my skin. "I long to claim you and to be claimed by you in return. Tell me you are mine, my beautiful Ashaya."

I cup his cheek and stare deep into his violet eyes. "I'm yours."

He leans in, seductively invading my mouth, devouring me with a passionate kiss that leaves me breathless and panting beneath him. He extends his claws into sharpened points, slicing a line down my leather tunic as he slides my pants off my hips.

His hands possessively trace over my body claiming me as his. He leans down and closes his mouth over my breast. The sensation of his sharp fangs as they scrape gently over the beaded tip sets my every nerve ending on fire. He continues down my body, my breath catching as he drags his tongue through my folds.

When he reaches the sensitive bundle of nerves at the apex, a low moan escapes me. I thread my fingers through his hair, holding him in place. Each movement of his tongue over my sensitive flesh is almost too much and yet, not enough all at once.

"Markus," I breathe. "Please."

I'm not even sure what I'm asking for as warmth pool deep inside my core.

"Your scent is intoxicating," he growls, and the vibrations move straight through me, igniting a spark deep within.

My entire body goes taut, and then bright light explodes behind my eyes as I come harder than I ever have before.

I'm not even fully recovered from my climax when he moves back up, lifting me into his arms. I inhale sharply as the crown of his stav bumps against my entrance.

I wrap my legs around his waist. "I want you, Markus," I breathe against his lips.

His gaze holds mine, and the breath stutters from my lungs as he slowly enters me.

Tight heat blooms in my core as he sheathes himself deep inside me. At first, it's uncomfortable like I've heard the first time can be, but after a moment, my body relaxes around him.

"So tight," he rasps as he begins to move deep inside me.

A soft moan escapes my lips as the ridges of his stav create the most delicious friction in my channel.

My toes curls with pleasure. The sensation of my body stretching around him is unlike anything I've ever felt before.

"You are mine," he groans as he wraps his wings tightly around me.

"Yours," I breathe.

He growls and changes the angle of his hips, sinking impossibly deeper inside me. Each movement of his stav in my channel brings me new pleasure.

His strokes become longer and deeper, and I'm lost in sensation as our bodies move as one. Nothing exists outside of this moment with him. Desire coils tight in my core with each thrust of his hips up into mine.

The small muscles of my channel begin to flex and quiver around his length as he quickens his pace. I hold tightly to him, digging my nails into his back as I chase my release.

He pulls back just enough to meet my eyes, his gaze full of fire and possession. "I want to give you my mark, Lara," he breathes against my lips.

I trust him. Completely. And because of that, I'm not afraid. I tilt my head to the side, offering him access to my neck. "Make me yours," I whisper.

He leans forward, and a moment later a slight sting pierces my skin at the curve of my neck and shoulder. It's followed quickly by intense pleasure.

He growls and each stroke becomes longer, deeper, and more forceful as he drags me closer to the edge.

I cling to his powerful form, feeling the strong muscles along his back flex beneath my fingers each time he thrusts into me, claiming me as his.

"Lara," he breathes my name out like a prayer as he continues to stroke into me. "Tell me you are mine, my beautiful Ashaya."

"Yours," I breathe. "Only yours."

Pleasure builds deep in my core as his strong body moves over mine. He tightens his wings around me, pulling me ever closer as each thrust become more powerful.

A low moan escapes me as my head falls back.

He grips my chin, and his violet gaze holds mine, full of fire and possession. "You are mine," he growls.

My mouth falls open and I cry out his name as wave after wave of pleasure moves through me. My climax triggers his own. He roars my name as his stav begins to pulse, and he erupts deep inside me, filling me with the delicious warmth of his seed.

It feels as if it goes on forever. The sensation sends me into another orgasm, this one even stronger than the last.

He seals his mouth over mine in a branding kiss and then rests his forehead against me as we remain joined, panting and locked together in an embrace.

His stav is still sheathed deep inside me as he lifts his gaze to mine. "Now, I will join our hearts and our souls as one, Lara."

My eyes drift down to his chest where his scales glow brightly. He extends his claws and pierces the scales over his heart, and the light begins to pulse even brighter.

He moves his hand to my chest, directly over my heart. His eyes meet mine. "I must pierce your skin to share my lifeforce with you."

"I trust you," I whisper.

His sharp claws lightly pierce my skin. A small hiss of pain escapes my lips at the slight sting, but he captures my mouth in a kiss, replacing my discomfort with pleasure.

He presses his chest to mine. Heat sears my skin directly beneath his beating heart, but he swallows my gasp with a kiss as warmth fills my chest, so intense I feel as if it is wrapping itself around my soul.

My body warms, and I hold him close, reveling in the sensation of being wrapped in layers of soothing warmth and protection.

I open my eyes in awareness as our hearts sync and begin beating in time as one. "You are my heart, Lara. We are one soul," he whispers before pressing a tender kiss to my lips.

"I love you, Markus," I breathe into his mouth. "I am yours."

A deep growl vibrates his chest at my words. He slides to his knees and wraps his arms and wings tightly around me, and begins stroking up into me again.

I whimper in ecstasy as he thrusts up into me like a man possessed, and it's all I can do to hold onto him, intense pleasure rippling through my entire body. He grips the long strands of my hair between his fingers and angles my lips to his. He plunders my mouth, swallowing my cries of passion as his stav pulses deep within, flooding me again with his essence.

I'm still coming as he bears me to the ground and begins to thrust into me.

I cup his cheek, barely managing to speak through my pleasure. "You already want me again?"

He presses his lips to mine and breathes against them. "Always, my Ashaya. I will take you many times this night." He stares down at me reverently, his gaze full of love and devotion. "You are mine, Lara, and I am yours."

CHAPTER 34

LARA

When I wake in the morning, every muscle in my body is sore, especially between my thighs, reminding me I've been thoroughly claimed by my mate. Markus nuzzles my temple. "I must have you again," he whispers.

He rolls me beneath him, groaning as he slowly enters my channel, fully seating himself deep inside me. A low moan escapes me with each stroke, longer and deeper than the last.

When I reach my climax, we fall over the edge together into blissful oblivion.

As we lie in bed, Markus tightens his wings around me, holding me close as he runs his fingers through my hair. He cups my chin, tipping my face up to his. "I am sorry I do not have more to offer you than this life."

I frown. "What are you talking about?"

"This place. This world." He gestures to the outside. "You deserve so much more than this. We have been trying to find a way off this world for the past five cycles; we have not given up. But I fear that we may be trapped here for many more cycles. Possibly even the rest of—"

I put my finger to his lips to silence him. "All we can do is try, Markus. We won't give up hope. Even if we are trapped here... at least we are free. It's not as if we have nothing. You still have technology. You've already built a home for you and your warriors."

"Two of our engineers have begun to carve out more rooms to accommodate your people," he adds. "We want to make sure they have their own quarters, if they wish."

Tears sting my eyes. He and his warriors are wonderful people. I'd worried they might not accept me because I am so different from them, but I am glad to know I was wrong.

I touch his face, tracing the sharp ridge of his brow as I stare deep into his gorgeous, violet eyes. "Even if we never leave this planet, that doesn't mean it can't be a home. The place we call home isn't as important as the people that are in it. As long as we're together, we can build a life."

He leans in and rests his forehead to mine. "Your words are wise. We will continue to search for a way to escape this world, but, in the meantime, we will build a life here... together.

"To be honest," I tell him. "I worry about what happens if or when we do leave this planet."

His brows pinch together in concern. "Why?"

"There are so many unknowns. I don't know how long I was in stasis sleep. My entire family might be gone already. And Vorek... he said your people don't take mates outside of your race. You're a Commander in the Mosauran Empire. Would your people accept—"

He silences me with a kiss. His tongue strokes against mine, stealing the breath from my lungs. When he finally pulls back, I'm breathless and panting.

He takes my hand and lifts it to his chest, directly over his heart. "You are my mate—my Ashaya. No matter what the future holds, know this: I vow that I will remain at your side for the rest of my days. The only thing that will ever tear us apart is the day that the Creator comes to take me from this world to the next. Even then... I would fight to stay with you."

Emotions lodge in my throat, but I somehow manage to speak around them. "I love you so much."

He brushes his lips against mine in a tender kiss. "You are my heart, Lara, and I am yours."

Markus carefully adjusts the leathers and furs around my body, and my heart melts at his efforts to make sure I'm completely covered and warm. His eyes flare with heat as they meet mine. "I already want to tear these from your body and take you again, my beautiful Ashaya."

"When we get to the springs, you can, my love."

He blinks several times then lifts me into his arms, rushing outside. Without bothering to shift into draken form, he takes off into the air so quickly I let out a small squeak of surprise.

When we land next to the springs, he quickly pulls away my many layers of clothing and walks me into the water. I twine my arms around his neck and press my lips to his as he wraps his arms and wings around my form.

His tongue curls around mine, deepening our kiss, until I'm breathless and panting. He notches his stav at my entrance then stills.

His head snaps toward the forest, and he quickly pulls me behind him, spreading his wings wide to shield me. My heart stops as he whispers urgently. "Someone is coming."

CHAPTER 35

MARKUS

My eyes go wide as one of my warriors comes rushing from the forest. He lands to the ground with a loud thump.

"Rokan found another Terran female." He lifts his wristband. "He contacted me and told me she is injured. He is flying her back to Healer Siran."

"How far away are they?"

He shakes his head. "I do not know. The signal cut off." His gaze darts to Lara. "Forgive me for intruding, but I scented that you were both nearby. I would have contacted you on my wristband, but it would not go through. But, I thought you would wish to know about the female."

"Thank you," Lara says. She turns to me. "We have to go! Now!"

When we reach our base. Lara and I rush to the med bay. As soon as we enter, we see the Terran female lying on one of the beds, Rokan at her side.

Lara takes her hand. "Emma? It's me, Lara."

She turns to face Lara and gives her a weak smile. "Lara," she whispers. "I'm so glad you're alive."

Lara looks to Healer Siran as he scans her. "Is she hurt?"

Siran nods, but Emma answers. "I'm just tired. That's all."

Siran studies his readout and gives Lara a grim look. "She has lost much blood"—he gestures to the two puncture wounds on her neck from an A'kai—"and she has several fractures, but I believe she will recover."

He turns to address Emma. "I must place you in the Med Repair Unit (MRU) for the fractures. The MRU will heal those, but the blood loss, I can do nothing about. We must wait for your body to replenish it naturally."

Rokan takes Emma's hand, and I watch as she squeezes it gently in return. "She is weak from the loss of so much blood. Is there nothing else you can do?" he asks, panic evident in his tone.

Lara holds out her arm to Siran. "Can you take some blood from me to give to her?"

He frowns, considering. "Yes. I could also possibly synthesize some so that I will not take too much from you. And because I have two samples to scan, it will give the machine more data to make certain it produces correctly."

He runs the scanner over them both then moves to one of his machines. While he is waiting for the synthesizer, Rokan's green eyes meet mine evenly. "The V'loryns have a Terran."

"You saw one with them?"

He shakes his head. "I could scent her. When I asked them about it, Commander Vorek became... aggressive. He demanded I leave."

"Aggressive?" I frown. "He knows we are searching for Terrans, and he knows we do not condone slavery. Why would he—"

"He claimed she is his *Si'an T'kara*. He thought I'd come to take her from him."

"What is a 'Si'an T'kara'?" Lara asks.

"A fated one," he explains. "It is equivalent to 'Ashaya,' in their culture."

Her lips part slightly. "Did he, at least, tell you her name?"

"Alana," he replies.

Lara's eyes brighten with tears. "Alana is my best friend; she's like a sister to me. We have to go get her, Markus."

I nod in affirmation. "We will. I will send one of our warriors to speak with the V'loryns about giving her over to us."

"Commander Vorek will not give her up," Rokan says. "She is his fated one."

"Do you think he's keeping her against her will?" Lara asks, worry etched in her features.

I take her hand. "The V'loryns are many things, but *this* I know they would not do. They do not condone slavery. They will not hurt your friend, nor would they hold her against her will."

"Even so," Lara says. "She's probably afraid. I mean… they look so much like the A'kai."

I dip my chin in understanding and move to the nearest control panel to activate the comms, requesting all our warriors to assemble near the wall.

I turn to Lara. "I will ask for a volunteer to travel to the V'loryn's territory. We will get your friend back."

Rokan's eyes lock with mine a moment, and it is easy to see the concern on his face. Commander Vorek's reputation as the fiercest Commander in the V'loryn fleet is known far and wide. We used to be friends once, and I pray he will listen to reason. He is not someone I wish to have as an enemy.

CHAPTER 36

LARA

When I wake in the morning, I go straight to the Med Center to check in on Emma. Rokan is there by her side, as he has been for the past few days.

I greet him warmly and take a seat on the opposite side of the bed to hold Emma's hand.

She smiles weakly up at me. "Hey," she barely manages.

"How are you feeling?"

"Better." She turns toward Rokan. "If Rokan hadn't saved me, I'd be dead."

"It's the same for me with Markus." I smile. "We've found more of our people."

"Yes," Rokan tells her. "Two of our warriors found three more. They are on their way here now."

A tear slips down her cheek. "Thank goodness. I was so afraid we were all that was left. What about Alana? Have you heard anything? Will the V'loryns let us see her?"

Rokan turns to her. "We've sent someone to speak with them."

"If they don't let them talk to her, Markus and I will go as well," I tell her.

"The V'loryns are good though, right?" She asks.

"Markus knows Commander Vorek. He won't hurt Alana. They aren't like the A'kai," I reassure her.

Warm hands come to rest on my shoulders and I tip my head back to see Markus. He leans down and presses a tender kiss to my forehead.

I'm so blessed that he was the one who found me. I know he says Vorek is a good man, but I still can't help but worry for my best friend.

I miss her and I can hardly wait to see her again.

EPILOGUE

LARA

As I lie snuggled up next to Markus, he places a tender kiss to my temple. He curls his body protectively around mine, wrapping his strong arms and wings around me.

It hasn't been very long, but it feels like forever since I met Markus. Even though we're stranded on an ice planet, I'm happier than I've ever been.

The engineers have already carved out several more rooms in the mountain for my people, when we find them.

Markus and I have discussed approaching the Lycaons to ask if they might want to share their crashed ship's technology. With their help, we might be able to repair at least one of our vessels. If it works, we could all escape this planet.

In the meantime, we leave tomorrow for the V'loryn territory to check in on Alana. Markus doesn't like the idea of me going, at all. He wants me to stay here, but I have to see my friend. I need to know she's all right. That she's happy where she is.

But, right now, I have something else I need to talk to him about. Healer Siran ran another scan on me and discovered something amazing.

Something that I know I certainly wouldn't have figured out for at least another month or two.

I lift my gaze to my Mosauran mate and take his hand in my own. "There's something I have to tell you."

His eyes search mine. "What is it?"

"I went to see Healer Siran this morning."

I place Markus's hand low on my abdomen.

His brow furrows, and I smile. "He says I'm carrying our fledgling."

"You are certain?" he asks. "Siran thought that medical intervention would be necessary to—"

"He was surprised too," I reply, remembering how big Siran's eyes were as he studied the readout. "He said he's sure, and that our fledgling is healthy."

Markus captures my mouth in a claiming kiss and then moves down my body. Gently, he nuzzles my stomach.

Running my fingers through his hair, a tear slips down my cheek as he lifts his violet eyes to mine, full of love and devotion.

"We will have a fledgling," he whispers. His gaze holds mine, and I note the flash of worry in his features when he reaches up to brush the tear away from my cheek. "Does this upset you?"

I take his hand, threading my fingers through his. "No, my love."

"Then, why are you crying?"

I smile warmly at him, then pull him up so his face is even with mine. "Because I'm so happy, Markus."

He presses his mouth to mine in a tender kiss.

He tightens his wings around me, pulling me closer. "You are my heart, Lara."

"And you are mine, Markus." I smile at him. "My ruggedly handsome, brave, and strong Mosauran warrior."

A devastatingly handsome grin lights his face as he rolls me beneath him. He brushes his lips over mine and then whispers against them. "Yours," he agrees.

ALSO BY JESSICA GRAYSON

The next book in the Ice World Warrior series is available here.
Vorek and Alana's story: Bound: Vampire Alien Romance

If you enjoyed this book, please leave a review on Amazon and/or Goodreads. If you enjoy my writing, I also write under the pen name *Aria Winter.*

Jessica Grayson

If you're curious about the *"Scarred Prince Soran of the Mosauran Empire"* his book is already available. **The Edge of it All**

Want more in this series ?

Ice World Warrior Series (Scifi Romance)

Claimed: Dragon Shifter Romance (This Book)

Bound: Vampire Alien Romance

Rescued: Fae Alien Romance

Stolen: Werewolf Romance

Taken: Vampire Alien Romance

Fated: Dragon Shifter Romance

Protected: Dragon Shifter Romance

Of Fate and Kings Series

Bound to the Dark Elf King

Claimed by the Dragon King

Taken by the Fae King

Stolen by the Wolf King

Captured by the Orc King

Check out some of my other books while you're here.

Do you like Fairy Tale Retellings?

Fairy Tale Retellings (Once Upon a Fairy Tale Romance Series)

[Taken by the Dragon: A Beauty and the Beast Retelling](#)

[Captivated by the Fae: A Cinderella Retelling](#)

[Rescued By The Merman: A Little Mermaid Retelling](#)

[Bound To The Elf Prince: A Snow White Retelling](#)

[Claimed By The Bear King: A Snow Queen Retelling](#)

[Protected By The Wolf Prince: A Red Riding Hood Retelling](#)

[Charmed by the Fox Prince: A Rapunzel Retelling](#)

Of Gods and Fate (Greek God Romance Series)

[Claimed By Hades](#)

[Bound to Ares](#)

Orc Claimed Series

[Claimed by the Orc](#)

[Bound to the Orc](#)

Night King Series

[Bound to the Night King](#)

Settlers of the Outer Rim

[Rescued: Fox Shifter Romance](#)

[Protected: Lizard Man Romance](#)

Fated to Monsters

[Captured by the Kraken: A Monster Romance](#)

[Bound to the Gargoyle: A Monster Romance](#)

[Claimed by the Werewolf: A Monster Romance](#)

Of Dragons and Elves Series (Fantasy Romance)

The Elf Knight

Scarred Dragon Prince Series

Shadow Guard: Dragon Shifter Romance

To Love a Monster Book Series (Fantasy Romance)

Taken by the Monster: A Monster Romance

Want Dragon Shifters? You can dive into their world with this completed Duology.

Mosauran Series (Dragon Shifter Alien Romance)

The Edge of it All

Shape of the Wind

V'loryn Series (Vampire Alien Romance)

Lost in the Deep End

Beneath a Different Sky

Under a Silver Moon

V'loryn Holiday Series (A Marek and Elizabeth Holiday novella takes place prior to their bonding)

The Thing We Choose

V'loryn Fated Ones (Vampire Alien Romance)

Where the Light Begins (Vanek's Story)

For information about upcoming releases Like me on

Facebook at Jessica Grayson

http://facebook.com/JessicaGraysonBooks.

OR

sign up for upcoming release alerts at my website:

Jessicagraysonauthor.com

www.ingramcontent.com/pod-product-compliance
Lightning Source LLC
Chambersburg PA
CBHW031955010726
47493CB00007B/2212